an **insiders** *girls* novel
^

# girls we love

# girls we love

## an insiders *girls* novel

by j. minter

BLOOMSBURY

**BLOOMSBURY**

Published by Bloomsbury Publishing, New York, London, and Berlin
Distributed to the trade by Holtzbrinck Publishers

Library of Congress Cataloging-in-Publication Data
Minter, J.
Girls we love : an insiders girls novel / by J. Minter. — 1st U.S. ed.
p.  cm.
Summary: While planning a sweet-sixteen party for Flan, who is not yet fourteen, the girls work on finally getting what they really want from their boyfriends, a group of wealthy Manhattan youths known as the Insiders.
ISBN-10: 1-58234-742-5 • ISBN-13: 978-1-58234-742-4
[1. Dating (Social customs)—Fiction.  2. Birthdays—Fiction. 3. Friendship—Fiction.  4. New York (N.Y.)—Fiction.]  I. Title.
PZ7.M67334Gir 2006      [Fic]—dc22      2006014397

Produced by Alloy Entertainment
151 West 26th Street
New York, NY 10001

First U.S. Edition 2006
Typeset by Westchester Book Composition
Printed in the U.S.A. by Quebecor World Fairfield
10 9 8 7 6 5 4 3 2 1

Bloomsbury Publishing, Children's Books, U.S.A.
175 Fifth Avenue, New York, NY 10010

All papers used by Bloomsbury Publishing are natural, recyclable products made from wood grown in well-managed forests. The manufacturing processes conform to the environmental regulations of the country of origin.

for MIG

**my name is flan**

Summer is supposed to be about sunbathing in grassy parks or rooftop gardens and window-shopping in the West Village with your girl-friends and obsessing over that big crush until one day he shows up at your house with a pretty bunch of yellow lilies. At which point, summer becomes all about making time to do all those things with him. Right? So then why was I, just days away from turning fourteen and a few measly weeks from being done with junior high forever, looking at summer and fearing that it was going to be a total wash?

Or, to put it another way, why had all my friends gone to Europe, or L.A., or suddenly decided that they were friends with high school sophomores who "really know how to party," or realized that they were East Village punkettes and stopped showering?

Or, to put it a third and last way, why, on the verge of what *should* be the most boy-packed summer of my life, was I sitting in my bedroom staring up at the wall collage of pictures of me and my very recent, very jerky ex, Remy Traubman? Remy was one of those guys who was six feet tall at eleven years old, and he has curly dark hair and olive skin, so he looks sort of like an Italian playboy or something even though he is so not. But you get the picture: He's cute and he knows it, and he doesn't bother hiding the fact that he thinks a lot of himself. All of which I realized after he stepped on my heart.

So there I was, on a perfectly beautiful Friday afternoon, in the most exciting city in the world (that would be New York, of course) mooning over these pictures of this guy with a head of hair that wouldn't be out of place on *America's Next Top Male Model*, if there were such a thing. This guy who had just dumped me in the most painful way possible.

Yeah, see, there was a real Italian playboy at our school this year, except that she was a play-girl, named Allegra Reggio, whose dad is like some international businessman or something. She's already started to do some modeling, but her parents wanted her to stay in normal school until she turned fifteen, which is how she ended up blessing us all with her presence. She always looked kind of like a starved child to me, but I guess Remy thought she was more glamorous or wild or fun or something than I was, because at some point we weren't going out anymore and it was obvious she was his girl.

I guess if I were somebody else, looking in through my bedroom window at me looking at these old pictures, seeing how sorry I was feeling for myself and all that, I might not think I was glamorous or fun to be around, either.

And just to really put some nail polish remover in that wound, as I was staring up at my unbearably dorky, and clearly made by a girl who was still thirteen, ex-boyfriend homage/wall decoration, I could hear the sounds of my older brother, Patch Flood, and his group of guys, having fun downstairs. They're all juniors at different private schools in the city, and they are always doing wild guy things like going to parties at three in the morning and exchanging one beautiful girl for another.

Oh, you've heard of them, right? Sometimes people call them the Insiders, but they always get all weird when they hear that.

Patch is like the aloof surfer dude among

them, and he's the guy who—I swear I don't think this just because he's my brother—the rest of them kind of wish they were. Maybe that's because he's self-sufficient, or lucky looking, or because he has our family's bone structure, but it's just kind of true. Mickey Pardo is the crazy one. He looks kind of like a Cuban Jack Black, but he's so charmingly screwed up that girls are always really into him. His father's a big famous sculptor named Ricardo Pardo, and my parents have all of this work of his up at our house in Connecticut. Arno Wildenburger is the hot, vain, dumb one, and David Grobart is the nice, quiet one, who is actually handsome if you look at him long enough.

And then there's Jonathan. I don't know which type he is, except that he always looks clean and put-together, and when his brown eyes look into your eyes, you feel like he's actually seeing you, and he is kind, but not boring kind, because you can talk to him about all sorts of random stuff. And I guess I should also say that he's the one who I kind of went out with for a little while way back at the beginning of the year.

They were all in the living room, and all the windows were open—I could tell by the level of noise coming from outside and floating up the trellis along with the ivy toward my bedroom window.

Me and Patch and my big sister, February, live in this really nice town house on Perry Street, filled with big, comfy, neutral-toned couches and lots of crazy modern art. Our parents live here, too, when they're in town. I know that sounds weird, but I'm the youngest of three New York City kids, so I guess when they got around to me they felt like they'd already seen it all and maybe didn't have anything to worry about so much anymore. So I kind of raised myself with help from Patch and Feb. Anyway, because our parents are up in Connecticut or traveling a lot, our house is perpetually the place to hang out.

So I listened to the guys, shouting about girls and making fun of each other and talking about all the great things they were going to do when school was finally out. My ex-boyfriend was on the wall, and my ex-ex-boyfriend was downstairs, and they were both more fun than I was.

I could have sat there feeling sorry for myself all day—if I'm being completely honest, it's happened before. But instead, I made a decision. I took a deep breath, and I promised myself that somehow, someway, fourteen was going to be bigger and better and wilder and more fun than thirteen. I swore to myself that once my birthday rolled by next week, I wasn't going to be the little sister that one of the guys used to sort of date anymore.

My name is Flan Flood. Don't forget it, okay?

I ripped down all those pictures of Remy. Surprise! It felt amazing. At first I was just ripping them off the wall, but then I got into it and started ripping them in half, and then ripping the half of the picture with him in it into smaller and smaller pieces. And, I'll admit it, I even yelped a little bit while I was doing it. I might have gone on doing this for hours—in fact, it might have gotten sort of psycho eventually—but my cell phone interrupted me.

See? You take one little self-respecting step like that, and all of a sudden you're a person to call.

"Hello?" I said.

"Hey, Flan? It's Liv," the voice on the phone said.

"*Liv* Liv?" I said. I could hardly believe it. Olivia Quayle was my best friend from elementary school, but I hadn't seen her in two years because she went to this super-elite boarding school in Montana, called the Cattington School, for seventh and eighth grade.

"Yeah, what other Liv do you know?" she said.

Kind of sharply, I thought, although clearly I was in a sensitive place what with all the ripping up of pictures. "I'm coming back to New York. Tomorrow. Can I stay at your house?"

"You want to stay at my house?"

"Yeah, my parents don't—I mean, they're in the Hamptons," she said, "and they don't want me staying by myself."

"Okay, but my parents aren't here, either," I said. "They're in Connecticut, I think."

"That's fine. Just so long as they don't think I'm alone."

"Oh, okay," I said. My first reflex was to be bummed, because after my big resolution to be more spontaneous and fun, hanging out with a friend from sixth grade didn't seem very bold, especially since Liv was kind of mousy when I saw her last. But then it dawned on me that, next to Liv, who had always been such a Goody Two-shoes—and I know this isn't nice, but yes, honestly, this is what was going through my mind—I was going to look cool. Like, fourteen- or maybe even fifteen-year-old cool. "Well, I'm so excited!" I said.

"Oh, me too," Liv said. "I'll call you tomorrow?"

"Okay," I said. "Kisses!"

"Kisses."

Then I hung up, and I realized that the wall above my bed looked really bare now, especially with a guest coming. So I thought about all the things I could put up there that would represent the new me—the me I was going to transform into—and then I knew what I should do. I took the free poster out of my new Leland Brinker CD, and taped it up, and then I got sort of creative and cut pictures of him out of different magazines and stuff. He's this really young singer-songwriter. Leland plays songs about staying up all night and then walking down New York City streets with the sun coming up and stuff, and he would be a senior in high school if he hadn't dropped out when he was fifteen. And I suddenly felt that he sang about the kinds of experiences the new me might have.

When I was done, I lay back on my bed and appreciated how much more sophisticated the room looked. I could still hear those guys, being all raucous downstairs, but I just lay there and smiled and waited.

Because sooner or later, they were going to meet the new me. My name is Flan, and this time around, I get to tell the story.

## i start planning for a big saturday night

For the old me, a movie worthy of my tears and mint chocolate chip ice cream would have been all I asked of my Saturday night. But since I was feeling a little sassy, and cleansed of the whole Remy thing, and since an old friend of mine was coming in from out of town in a couple of hours, I thought I'd ask my older brother, Patch, what was going on that night.

Patch's clique of guys gets talked about all the time, and invited to like every party worth going to, even though really he just likes riding the subway and seeing random stuff happen and eating real Mexican food in Queens and places like that. But because of his friends, and also because (I have to admit) he's kind of magnetic, Patch is always being quasi-forced into Saturday night madness. I thought I'd try to get him to tell me where *the* party was going to be, so I could take Liv and the new me there.

Also, girls really love hanging out with Patch, even girls like Liv who wear turtlenecks and other lumpy clothing items, so I figured it would be kind of a treat for her if we ended up hanging out with him. He's my brother, so I try really hard not to think about this, but lots of other people think he's dreamy, too, so I've had to become immune to that kind of talk. It's the same with my sister, February. People are always saying how totally bats she is and I'm immune to hearing that, too. But I do understand that she's bats—the family doesn't try to hide anything from me anymore.

It was one of those lazy, almost summer vacation days, when nothing really happens until the sun goes down. Liv called at four-thirty, when she was in the cab on the way from LaGuardia, to make sure I was planning something. "Flan?" she yelled from her cell phone. "I forgot how freakishly ugly and untamed this city is. I'm so excited! We're going out, right?"

"Definitely," I said, even though I still didn't know where. I wasn't worried, though. I figured just leaving the house and getting Mary's Dairy frozen yogurt would be a trip, especially after two years in Montana. But I wasn't going to settle for that just yet.

I went down to the living room, where Patch was drinking beers with his friend Arno, who might be cute if he weren't so full of himself. They were watching *Kung Fu Hustle* for like the zillionth time. They were both wearing T-shirts and jeans, although Patch's looked like, you know, a T-shirt and jeans, whereas Arno's outfit looked like something a team of stylists spent two days choosing for somebody's first gig at the Bowery Ballroom.

"Hey, Flan," Arno said, cocking his eyebrow in my direction in this way that totally made me feel my age. Even though I know Arno is kind of a jerk, he's still really pretty, and he makes me nervous even when I'm trying to force myself not to be. "You want a beer?"

My older brother and his friends always let me have beers, but Arno has to do this whole show of teasing me about it first. I tried to give him a sarcastic little smile as I reached over and grabbed a PBR, but I'm not very experienced with that sort of thing yet, so it might not have worked.

Patch gave Arno a don't-be-a-dick face, and then he said, "What's up, Flannie?"

"Nothing much," I said, sitting down on the floor with my knees tucked underneath me. As soon as I was sitting, I realized that this meant I was looking up at my brother and Arno, who were sprawled across the couch all guy-like. Mental note: When attempting to transform into a party girl, try *not* making yourself look so small all the time.

"I heard you just broke up with some junior high kid," Arno said.

"What?" I said, really hoping that he didn't notice my ears getting all hot and red. My dumping by Remy was absolutely the last thing I wanted to talk about with an older guy, even if I have known him forever.

"Arno, shut up," Patch said.

"Sorry, Flan," Arno said, and he actually kind of looked like he was. "I didn't mean that to sound mean." He sighed. "And I like your dress."

"Thanks," I said, looking down at the yellow cotton sleeveless sundress that I've been wearing like every day since the weather got warm. I waited a minute, and then asked, "So . . . what are you guys doing tonight?"

Patch thought about it, and then said, "Something, I guess, I don't know."

"Yes you do," Arno shot back.

My brother gave his friend a blank look, and then Arno kept talking like he was telling Patch something painfully obvious. "Tonight is Liesel Reid's sweet sixteen party, don't you remember?"

"Oh . . . that uptown girl you were fooling around with last winter?" Patch asked. Then he went quiet and we waited for him to say whatever he was going to say next. He does this thing when he says people's names—I don't think he even knows he does it, but it always makes people feel special. He took a deep breath and said, "Huh. Liesel Reid. Why do we have to go to her sweet sixteen party?"

"Because for some reason she invited me, and I said I would go, and then all of you promised you would come with me." Arno slumped on the couch, letting his very expensively cut mop of dark hair fall in his eyes. "But if that's too much to ask, whatever. I mean, I was trying to be a bigger person, but I guess nobody cares."

"Fine," Patch said. "We'll go to Liesel Reid's sweet sixteen tonight." He turned to me, and smiled like he was letting me in on the joke. "I guess we're going to Liesel Reid's sweet sixteen party tonight. It's probably at the Boat House in Central Park."

"It is," Arno, who was not yet totally out of pout mode, said.

"Oh, perfect—I mean cool." I tried to take a dainty sip of my beer, which is, by the way, a really tricky thing to do. "Can I come? And maybe bring a friend?"

Both Patch and Arno turned in my direction, stared for a minute, and then said, "Okay."

"Great!" I said, clapping my hands together because I love the Boat House, and all of this sounded much more fun than some house party with loud music and obnoxious people. "I'll go get dressed." I put down the beer, glad that I had something to do, because I was sort of hating drinking it.

"It's not till, like, nine," Arno said, sounding just like the pretty, not-very-bright guy who'd been teasing me about drinking beer a few minutes ago.

"Oh, okay. Sure," I said, and then they went back to watching the movie and I went out front because I heard a cab pulling up in front of the house.

I stood on the stone steps and watched as the cabdriver took three really big suitcases out of the trunk and put them on the sidewalk. Then Liv got out of the backseat and paid him and came running up and threw her arms around me.

"Oh my God, it's so good to see you!" she squealed.

"You too," I said, and then I couldn't help but say, "You look amazing!"

And she did, too. She had gotten really tall and chesty and her skin was all golden from being out west. Liv used to be this girl with frizzy hair and a mouth that was freakishly large, but now it was like she had grown into her face, and the size of her mouth and the cat eyes—the whole thing just worked. Evidently somebody in Montana really knew how to do awesome-looking highlights, too. I guess I shouldn't have been surprised. I've grown in all those ways, too, except for the skin tone part, since no matter what I do I'm really pale, but still, it's weird when you haven't seen somebody in a while and note how they've changed and gotten all . . . sexy looking.

Especially if that person used to wear maroon turtlenecks.

"You think so? Wow, thanks. I mean horse-back riding is so different in the west and you know . . ." Liv kept talking while we hauled her huge bags up to my room. It didn't even occur to me how much stuff this was, because we had so much catching up to do.

We talked the whole time we were getting ready to go, and even though Liv had brought three suitcases of clothes, she ended up wearing this powder blue scoop neck C&C California shirt of mine with a jeans miniskirt I've had forever. I ended up sticking with my yellow sundress, but I put on a double strand of my mom's pearls and put my hair in a twist so it would be a little more beach-girl-goes-formal. I told her all about Remy, and what a dick he ended up being, and she told me all about her boyfriends at the Cattington School. Her many, many boyfriends.

Getting dressed really can be the best part of the night sometimes, and when it was time to go I was almost disappointed. But that's maybe just me being a little shy.

Anyway, at some point Arno knocked on my door and then poked his face in and told us the ship was leaving. Liv gave me this OMG-he's-cute look, and then we took big breaths and followed him outside.

We were in a cab, cruising uptown, when I said, "Hey Patch, where are the rest of your friends?"

Arno turned around in the front seat to look at

Patch, and then Patch said, "We're meeting all of them there."

"Oh, okay," I said, trying not to sound like I cared too much. Which I didn't, although I did want to be . . . prepared, I guess, in case Jonathan ended up there, too. He can be annoyingly, like, knowing about stuff sometimes, but in some ways I suspect he's my best friend, or maybe soul mate, which makes it all the more weird that I haven't hung out with him in so long.

I stared out the window for a lot of blocks and had a lot of thoughts about Jonathan and how difficult he was and how we argued all the time but also kind of enjoyed watching TV together in my parents' bed when they weren't around. And that's basically all the time, as I've mentioned.

At the corner of Fifth and Seventy-second there were a bunch of carriages in a row. This driver wearing a top hat over a kind of gross ponytail asked us if we were there for the Reid affair. I would *so* ride around Central Park in carriages all the time if the drivers weren't so weird and kind of dirty.

"Yes, unfortunately," Arno said to the ponytail guy.

"What?" Patch said. "I thought you were all psyched on this."

"Well, we've all been hired to drive you to the Boat House. So get on in," the ponytail guy said, ignoring Patch and Arno. Liv and I climbed up first, and then my brother and his friend followed.

"This is so much fun," Liv said. I nodded in agreement, but I guess she wasn't talking to me, because she added, "Patch, isn't this fun?"

"I guess so," Patch said. "Actually, I don't know if I've ever been in one of these before."

As we rode into the quiet leafiness of the park, we started to overtake another carriage with some other partygoers in it. I knew they were going to the same place, because their carriage was decorated with the same big pink bows as ours was.

"Hey," Arno said, loud enough for them to hear, "don't we know those kids?"

There were two boys and a girl in the carriage, and they all turned to look.

"Wait a minute," Liv said, in a voice that was maybe supposed to be quiet but definitely was not. "Flan, isn't that that guy Jonathan you used to be secretly in love with?"

Everyone was staring at me, and maybe I would have been embarrassed, except that I was really distracted by this strange thing Jonathan was doing. Which was that he totally had his arm around some girl with shiny brown hair and a lot of freckles who was smiling idiotically at us like we were all about to be her new best friends.

I mean, what was that about? And when did Liv become so totally tactless?

## everyone has to talk to the new girl, and
## tonight the new girl's name is liv

"Hey, did I meet you at the Yale Early Action meeting last week?"

Liv Quayle tossed her long, wavy hair over her shoulder and took a look at the latest guy to approach her. He was tall, with slicked back hair, and he was wearing a blazer and smiling wolfishly. He looked pretty uptown. Most of the guys at the party were pretty uptown.

"I don't think so," Liv said, smiling conspiratorially at her crew of new friends, Jonathan, Ava, Arno, and David. Her best friend from elementary school, Flan, was standing with them, too. But Flan was a bit off to one side, looking just slightly piqued. "Especially since I haven't even started high school," Liv added, in order to bring home to this guy that he was absolutely no Patch Flood.

Because that was the guy she was holding out for

tonight. And she could wait—she had spent two long years in Montana keeping her love for him, which dated to third grade, a secret. It wasn't until her last e-mail from good ol' Flan hinted at how big and popular he'd gotten recently that she realized it was time to come back to New York and make her love for him real. It was perfect timing, because she had finally gotten all hot and popular, too.

"Oh," the uptown guy said, looking a little confused, like he wasn't sure whether to keep hitting on her or scamper away. "Um, I guess it was nice to meet you then," he said, and lifted his glass at her before turning around.

Liv wiggled her fingers in his direction, and mouthed *Buh-bye* at his back as he moved through the topiaries and white balloon sculptures set up throughout the Boat House restaurant. The beamed ceilings over their heads were decorated with strands of Christmas lights arranged in cursive L-shapes, and out the windows they could see a warm summer night descending on the park. Their little group had been enjoying rounds of pink champagne from the trays being circulated by waiters. And Liv was getting increasingly weak-kneed by the general madness infiltrating the usually staid restaurant.

"This really isn't my regular scene," Liv said with a giggle, to no one in particular. What she meant of course was that it was filled with guys who were cute but totally uninteresting compared with Patch, who was even more sparkly-eyed and delicious than when she got sent away to boarding school by her parents.

But she couldn't think about them now. If she thought about her parents she would have to admit to herself that they were probably wondering where she was right now, and then she would have to deal with that. For Liv, ignorance-is-bliss had always been a friendly motto.

She took a sip of her champagne and surveyed the crowd. There were a number of older women with big dramatic hats, though the place was jam-packed with kids, too, most of whom looked pretty preppy but also looked like they knew how to party. Whoever this Liesel girl was, she had really gone all out. Downtown-famous DJ Tahoe was spinning, which had inspired a small but enthusiastic dance floor in the corner. He was playing a Kanye West song, and a bunch of kids were getting down quite a bit farther than Liv would've thought they could.

"It's not my scene, either," Jonathan said emphatically. He was wearing a light brown suede motorcycle jacket and his bangs were styled diagonally across his forehead as though he were an actor playing a private-school boy on TV. "This place was built in what, 1910?"

"I like the Boat House," the Ava girl with all the freckles said. She had a big smile on her face. "I think it's really classic. And I think it's much older than that."

"Mmmhhmm," Liv said, rolling her eyes. Liv had decided that Jonathan was totally cute, and Ava was totally not. She leaned over to Flan and whispered, "He is so darn cute. For you, I mean." Flan evidently agreed, because she jabbed her elbow into Liv's side in excitement/horror.

Two guys wearing blazers and gigantic chrome watches walked by and gave Liv the up and down.

"It must make you sort of uncomfortable that all these guys are hitting on you," Patch's friend David said. He was really tall. David was obviously not a guy who had ever been very smooth with girls and probably wouldn't know fun if it came over and yanked down his baggy jeans.

"No, I've gotten used to it," Liv said. Then she laughed (being careful not to shoot champagne through her nose, which was so something she would have done two years ago, except with milk) just to show that she didn't take her new hotness too *too* seriously.

"Oh, okay," David said. Liv gave him a pitying smile, because she could tell he wanted her a little bit, and then she craned her neck for Patch. He'd been kind of oblivious to the fact that they were about to begin the most important romance of their young lives, which of course made him totally all the more irresistible.

A new song came on, and Flan grabbed Liv by the arm, in this weird awkward way that made Liv wonder if maybe Flan wasn't a little jealous of the new, hot Liv. "Let's dance!" she said really loudly, and started pulling her away from the other kids.

"No, wait," Liv said. "Where's your brother? Let's get him first. He loves to dance, right?" She looked around, and realized that Patch, who had been standing so quietly and patiently, had finally snuck off to some secret place, probably hoping that she would watch him go and then follow a few minutes later. But she had totally missed it, and now she had no idea where he was or even which direction he might have gone in. Damn!

"Um, not really," Flan was saying. She widened her big blue eyes at Liv in a way that made Liv wonder if something was wrong. Like, maybe Flan was trying to tell her that she had lipstick on her teeth?

"Patch definitely doesn't like to dance," Arno said, kind of sarcastically. Liv made a mental note: Her dream man did not like to dance. "Hey, where'd he go anyway?"

Jonathan and David shrugged. "We should be used to Patch disappearing by now," Jonathan said.

"I'll dance with you, Liv," Arno said, stepping forward.

"Oh my God!" Liv shrieked, pretending not to hear

Arno's offer. He was cute, too, of course, but she had to keep her eyes on the prize. "Look, you guys, you see that girl in the big movie star glasses over there? I think that's Sara-Beth Benny." She looked at the group, waiting for them to recognize the starlet and be as excited as she was. "You know, from that old TV show *Mike's Princesses*—do you recognize her?"

"That's not her," Arno said, arching an eyebrow dubiously in the direction of the girl hiding behind the sunglasses. She had a dramatic black bob, and she looked very tiny making her way through the crowd. "I know SBB. And so does David. And that's totally not . . . David?"

They all turned toward David, but David had scurried away in the other direction.

"That's weird," Jonathan said. "I think that maybe *is* SBB. No one else could have made David bolt like that."

"You know her?" Liv gushed. "She is like my style icon. Can we meet her?"

Jonathan shrugged. "I guess, if you really want, but don't tell David. He's still pretty messed up about how she moved into his parents' house and morphed from his girlfriend into his sister."

"Gross," Liv said, wrinkling her nose. "I still want to meet her, though. Flan, don't you *totally* want to meet her?"

Flan looked like she wasn't sure for a minute, and

25

then a smile broke through on her face. "Okay," she said, "I totally want to meet her, too."

Jonathan smiled, and Liv was pretty sure there was some kind of connection between him and Flan. Liv resolved to give Flan whatever help she needed. That way, once it came out that Liv and Patch were like this hot super couple, Flan and Jonathan could be like their slightly-less-golden-couple friends. "All right, ladies," Jonathan said, bringing Liv back down from her Patch fantasy. "But prepare yourselves. That one has got some real emotional problems."

"Yeah," Arno said. "She's like the most needy person ever, and she apparently will recite whole episodes of that old TV show she was on for anybody who asks. All that stuff about her passing out at weird bars and going to, like, Thailand at the drop of a hat . . . it's all true."

"Really?" Liv said, wishing she knew what Thailand looked like. "That's so cool."

Ava made a face. "This feels kind of exploitative. I'm just going to stay here, okay?" she said, like she thought they were all being celebrity whores.

Jonathan looked sort of exasperated or confused or something and then he said, "Okay," and turned back toward Flan and Liv. They all looked to where Sara-Beth Benny had been, but by then the whole room had shifted. The crowd had parted at the middle, and people were pushing at them to move back from the center.

The music had changed, too; DJ Tahoe had been replaced by a quartet of classical musicians playing some very dramatic piece.

Liv turned toward the entryway, and that was when she saw a white horse cantering into the restaurant. The horse had a big pink bow around its neck and on its back was a tall, slender girl with thoroughbred cheekbones and a mane of ash-blond hair rising from her forehead. She was wearing a white eyelet Michael Kors dress that buttoned all the way from the ankle to the bust and had a prairie shirt collar, and she was smiling and waving like a princess.

"Oh my God," Flan said, clapping her hands, "isn't that horse beautiful?"

Liv clapped, too, because she was witnessing the sort of wattage you just don't get out west. She felt like every moment she spent in New York, she was learning a little bit more about how to win Patch and then keep him in her clutches forever.

When the big white horse came riding through the Boat House, Sara-Beth Benny breathed a sigh of relief. Now, finally, people would stop staring at her and wondering if she was who they thought she was. Or whether or not she'd had lunch. Or dinner.

She wouldn't even have gone out, except that she had to find David Grobart. And some sixth sense had told her that David Grobart would be at the Boat House tonight. Which was a nice coincidence, because the Boat House was where her mother had always taken her for lunch as a little girl when they were in New York. Sara-Beth's mother was a famous stage actress who retired at thirty-three to marry the CEO of a telecommunications company, and always regretted it, and when she took her only daughter to the Boat House they would bond by ordering their hamburgers well-done and then sending them back to the kitchen for being burned. Mom loved the Boat House almost as much as Sara-Beth did, but she wouldn't come to New York anymore because she insisted that everyone just looked at her and whispered *failure* under their breath. That was why SBB lived in a New York apartment by herself, and only went back to her parents' Los Angeles home for holidays. But she didn't really like being in her cold, lonely apartment, which was one of the reasons why she had to find David Grobart. His parents, who were therapists, had taken her in and let her live with them before her last business trip to Los Angeles.

So she had put on a shapeless dress made out of burlap that she'd bought in this little boutique on Mott Street, and a black wig that she had worn in one of the last episodes of *Mike's Princesses,* the TV show that had made her famous. She'd worn the wig in the episode where she and her sisters suspected that their single dad might be dating their school principal, and trailed him in disguise.

She was pretty sure that people were still staring at her. A-holes!

SBB pushed against several of them as she moved out into the crowd, and hoped that the burlap would scratch them.

There was some to-do in the middle of the room—

a guy in a bow tie who evidently worked at the Boat House was sweating and pleading with Liesel Reid, resplendent on top of a white horse, to get down.

"Miss Reid," he was saying, "animals of a certain size are simply not allowed in our establishment. Now, you are a very special guest, but I'm still going to have to . . ."

Liesel Reid shook her mane of ash-blond hair and continued to blow kisses at her friends, who were all jumping up and down and calling out her name. SBB was glad to see Liesel even if she was surrounded by adoring fools. The girls had known each other since kindergarten, when they had gone to the same school, and they understood each other. SBB pushed past the bow-tie man, consciously trying to scratch him with her dress, and grabbed on to the horse's saddle. The horse snorted and shifted nervously in the crowd.

"Liesel," she hissed.

Liesel took a look at the pint-sized girl standing below her, and then gave her a bland smile and a cupped-hand wave. A beat later, she realized who was hiding under those big glasses.

"Oh my God, SBB!" she shrieked.

Sara-Beth gave a fierce little shake of her head and put a finger over her lips, which she had used an almost white shade of lipstick on.

Liesel shifted her tan, well-defined jaw, and realized

her mistake. She rotated and waved at the crowd. After the moment had passed, she leaned over slickly and blew kisses on either side of Sara-Beth's face. "I'm so glad you could make it," she said. "I haven't seen you since the Mawc Jacobs show."

"That catastrophe," Sara-Beth said from behind her Marc shades. "They put us in the second row."

"Idiots," Liesel said happily. "Anyway, why the wig? New look for you. Very Uma circa *Pulp Fiction*."

"I'm undercover," Sara-Beth said, looking about her furtively to make sure that no one was listening. Luckily, everyone was busy discussing how gorgeous Liesel looked. Even Mr. Bow Tie had run away for backup. "I've just been on the coast, and guess what! I got a part in that genius indie director Ric Rodrickson's new movie. It's due to start shooting in Gdańsk in ten days, and it's in my contract that I'm not supposed to be partying."

Liesel and Sara-Beth exchanged simultaneous eye rolls.

"Anyway, great party. We should catch up once you come down off the horse."

"I would love that," Liesel said, making the call-me gesture with her hand, and squeezing her heels into her horse's sides. Then the horse moved into the crowd, with Liesel extending her hands down for people to touch as though she were a princess or a rock star. Or a little bit of both.

Sara-Beth moved with hunched shoulders and downcast eyes through the crowd. She tried to imagine that she was in character . . . as a hobo. She spotted David's friends standing near the dance floor, but David wasn't with them, and Sara-Beth decided that it would be too much of a to-do if she tried to say hi to all those people. They were cool kids, but even they couldn't help getting sort of starstruck around her. She was, after all, a star.

She slipped along the wood-paneled walls, smiling at waiters and generally trying not to be noticed. All of the air-kissing and music and hellos and all the food smells were sort of getting to her, though, and she was struck by a sudden panic that maybe she looked more SBB-like than she realized.

She swiveled in the other direction and headed for the bathroom, trying to hide her face with her hand. That's when she saw him.

He was standing against a wall and looking around warily, all six foot five of him, and his hair was a dark shadow on a nearly shaved scalp. David Grobart was, without a doubt, her hero. He was even wearing under-cover garb that must've been meant to be sympathetic to her—a regular navy hoodie and nondescript jeans and plain old basketball shoes.

SBB spread her arms back against the wall and moved in. Meanwhile David pretended not to notice her. When she reached him she did a little spin and landed against his chest. Before he could say anything, she put her finger across his lips.

"You're going to make such a good prison guard," she whispered.

David's face did a number of confused contortions.

"I missed you so much," Sara-Beth went on. "But now we're going to be together all summer on the movie set! In Gdańsk. We'll probably live in a little tent together and cook meals on an open fire . . ." SBB paused, remembering she had never cooked anything, and that she'd never seen her mother cook anything, either. "Or maybe it'd be better if we got someone else to do that . . ."

SBB was feeling all kinds of emotions, and she knew the small, soft tip of her nose was probably bobbing with feeling. Directors kept telling her not to do this, but she couldn't help it. Finally, in Ric Rodrickson, she had found a director who liked what her nose did.

"Don't look at me that way, I know I'm not making any sense," Sara-Beth said, leaning her face against David's chest so that she couldn't see his face.

"I'm just confused," he said. "I mean, you just disappeared . . . and now you're back."

"I was in L.A., meeting a director, and now I'm going to star in a moo . . . film. And you're coming with me! I got you a part and everything! As a prison guard."

She pressed herself against David again, happily indulging herself in his warmth and bigness. When she looked back up at him she was met by blank eyes and a face that looked sort of freaked out.

"David?" she wailed. "You're upset, aren't you. I know, I know. I didn't think the prison guard part was right, either. We'll do better. I'll make Ric come up with something amazing for you to do." She put her head back against his chest. "But David? The important thing is we're together. Right? David?"

## sad, but true: every girl wants to control her ex's future love life

"Is that what I think it is?" Philippa Frady's girl-friend of a few months muttered disgustedly when she saw the white horse. Her name was Stella, and she was a junior at Barnard. "This is like some bizarre, candy-coated 1950s fantasy of girlhood." Stella's eye had begun to twitch. "If you'll excuse me."

Philippa watched as her older girlfriend flipped open her phone and walked over to a corner of the restaurant to make a call. Stella had been making calls all day. She had severe features and wore a stiff-collared shirt, and she always did things with a deter-mined seriousness. Right now, she was probably calling the Barnard paper to report pre-feminist doings. She was their art critic.

When Philippa was sure that Stella was out of sight, she turned and giggled apologetically at the couple they had come to Liesel Reid's sweet sixteen with. Liesel was a friend of hers from elementary school, before Philippa's parents left their natural setting, the Upper East Side, for the West Village. "I really like the Boat House," she said softly. "Don't tell Stella, though, okay?"

She'd meant it as a joke, but Mickey Pardo, her last boyfriend as a straight person, and Sonya Maddox, this bi girl she'd met at Starlight, didn't laugh. Sonya had seemed like a good potential playmate for Mickey, because when Philippa first saw her she was dancing on the bar to that unbearably catchy Kelly Clarkson song, and Philippa knew from personal experience that Mickey liked that sort of thing. So she played matchmaker.

Plus, Philippa had been brought up with manners, and it just seemed like good manners to make sure your ex was taken care of once you'd moved on. Even if he was sort of trouble, and even if her parents were really uptight and had never approved of him in the first place. But the loyalty she felt toward Mickey went way back, and it was hard to just stop feeling a thing like that.

As far as Philippa was concerned it was a perfect setup. By double-dating, she and Mickey could hang out free of any of the lingering tension from their long-term relationship, and plus, Sonya could be her new bi/queer-friendly buddy. Mickey had only met Sonya three hours ago and they already seemed to be talking to each other with their eyes the way couples do. Philippa sensed that they had already planned out a whole summer of antics, and she wasn't sure why this made her feel weird.

"Whatever," Sonya said, tossing her long, straight, dyed-black hair over her shoulder. "She's just pissed 'cuz she doesn't get to ride the horse."

Sonya had thin lips, piercing blue eyes, long, dirty-blond roots, a very high forehead, and a pink face, and she was wearing a jeans skirt and a wife-beater. Her outfit made her look tough, but also like a girl who just wanted to have fun. Philippa could tell just from looking at her that she smoked a lot of pot.

"Lesbians." Mickey rolled his eyes and then instinctively protected his chest with his arms. Sonya's and Philippa's punches landed hard. "Hey, I'm outnumbered. Quit it!"

Then Philippa ruffled Mickey's thick, dark hair affectionately, and forgot that she had come to the party with somebody else. It was only earlier that year that she'd come out to Mickey and then broken up with him. They had gone out for years, so she still had brief lapses of relationship amnesia.

Sonya put her inexplicably athletic body against Mickey and kissed him. Philippa caught a little glimpse of tongue. That jogged her memory.

"Anyway," Philippa said, to remind them she was still there, "I think the horse is really pretty."

"Oh, me too," Sonya said, pulling her mouth away

from Mickey but leaving her arm draped around his shoulder. "I would definitely ride it."

Mickey was shorter than all his friends, and stocky almost, and Sonya was wearing high wedge heels, so she was a few inches taller than him. Philippa had paired ballet flats with her Built by Wendy madras summer dress—it was still sort of her habit to wear shoes that kept her shorter than Mickey. She noticed for the first time that Mickey, under his basic Dickies cutoffs and white T-shirt, was wearing white clogs. Improbably, he looked cute in them.

"What do you think is going on over there?" Mickey asked.

"Some kind of big to-do," Philippa said, raising her arched eyebrows in the direction of the white horse, which was now moving restlessly amid all the confusion at the center of the crowd.

"Whoa, that little man with the bow tie is turning all tomatolike," Mickey said.

"He agrees with your girlfriend, apparently," Sonya said, smiling at Philippa. "Horses are definitely a pre-feminist fantasy of—"

"Oh, hold up," Philippa said, pretending like she hadn't heard the reference to her girlfriend. If they all kept dwelling on it she thought she might cry. And also, she knew that her girlhood had basically been of the pre-feminist sort, and she wanted to keep the conversation clear of that. "Look at that. Liesel's totally yelling back."

"Damn," Mickey said. "I would not want that chick yelling at me. That's that crazy preppy girl Arno was hooking up with last winter. The one who always sounds like she's talking baby talk."

"Um, yeah? It's her party, Mickey," Philippa said impatiently.

"Right, right," Mickey said. "Hey, look! She's getting down off the horse."

"I love how she's wagging her finger at the bow-tie dude. That's out of control!" Sonya laughed. She had a deep, throaty laugh. "Oh my God, she's really telling him off."

Liesel Reid did indeed appear to be pissed off, and all the people around her were staring at the bow-tie man in a kind of menacing way, too. "I sort of feel for that guy, actually. Liesel really knows how to throw a fit," Philippa said. "I was with her at Saks once, and the gift-wrap girl forgot to clip the tag . . . it was brutal."

"Oh, whatever. She's just going to tell him he ruined her party and he's going to grovel and later her family will tip him double." Sonya shrugged. "What I'm worried about is the horse. I'm a vegan."

Later, Philippa would return to that moment as the beginning of her questioning the wisdom of matchmaking.

"Wait a minute . . ." Mickey said. He said it kind of slowly, like an idea was coming to him. Then he leaned over and whispered into Sonya's ear. Her mouth opened slightly like she'd been told something unbelievable and grand, and then she nodded vigorously. "Okay, c'mon," Mickey said, grabbing her hand and dragging her into the crowd. "Catch you later, sister," he called behind him. Sonya gave Philippa a thumbs-up and mouthed *thank you* as she followed Mickey in Liesel's direction.

Philippa watched as Mickey and Sonya weaved through the crowd, which was looking a little drunk by now. Mickey was always pulling these dangerous, crazy stunts—when they had first started going out it seemed exciting, but then it felt scary, and then after that just sort of old. Now, watching him slip through all those loud, buzzed people to lift this other girl up onto a horse, Philippa was struck by how fun it looked.

"Sorry," Stella said. Philippa turned to see that her girlfriend had returned and was standing right behind her. "I had to make that," Stella said as she slipped her cell phone into her trousers pocket.

"No problem," Philippa said. She could never help but be impressed by Stella, who was always thinking of things that had to be said out loud and getting calls that she had to take.

"Where'd Mickey and Sonya go?"

"Um, they—" Before Philippa could say anything else, a collective gasp reverberated through the crowd. She turned and saw Mickey and Sonya on the back of the big white horse. Which was charging through the Boat House.

"Oh my God," Philippa whispered gleefully. She heard Mickey yell "Adios, suckers" just before the horse made it to the front door and disappeared in a flash of white. She turned to her girlfriend, expecting to see an expression of awed disbelief.

Stella smiled a deeply sarcastic smile. "Are we having fun yet?" she said in a tone that seemed designed to kill any possibility of fun.

## liesel reid on the meaning of fate

"Look, you let them steal my hawsie!" Liesel Reid shouted at Georges Langley, the manager of the Boat House, who was supposed to be making sure her sweet sixteen party was fabulous. Thus far, she didn't think he was doing an especially good job. "Are you trying to ruin my party?"

"Miss Reid," Georges stammered. "You don't seem to understand—"

"I mean, do you know who my family is? Or who I wuhk for? I may be in high school, but I've been in PR for two semesters now, so if you think . . ." Liesel might have gone on, except that she noticed that Georges's bow tie was pathetically askew. And anyway, yelling at a short, paunchy, middle-aged restaurant manager was beneath her, and so she huffed, and turned on her Louboutin heels. "Nevah mind, Georges," she called over her shoulder as she headed for the bathroom to fix herself up.

Liesel was tall and pale, with the boyishly skinny body of an Eastern European runway model, and the kind of bone structure that screamed old money. Her parents were famous art collectors, and she was used to being stared at. But she also knew a thing or two about grace, which was why she was striding through a crowd of her enthusiastic friends and admirers and past the long bathroom line to splash some water on her face, wash off every bit of that unpleasant encounter, and put her charm back on.

When she reached the head of the line she smiled sadly at a girl in a sweater set and headband, who was pressing her knees together and gritting her teeth, and said, "You understand."

"Of course, Liesel," the girl said sweetly.

"You'll make sure nobody comes in?"

The girl nodded, and then Liesel pushed through the door.

She was carefully reapplying the mascara that brought out the cornflower blue of her especially round, especially wide eyes, when the door swung open.

"Hey, wait," Liesel said, swiveling around from the mirror. When she saw who it was, her face brightened. "Oh, Awno!"

"Hey, Liesel," he said softly. That was weird. Arno Wildenburger was not known for his soft voice. He was six feet tall—exactly as tall as Liesel, which was only one of several reasons that they had always seemed like the perfect couple that hadn't quite happened yet. He had the kind of just-exotic-enough features that made it hard for a girl to stop picturing his face when she was kissing other guys. He was really downtown, and Liesel liked that about him.

"What are you doing here?" she asked. "We're pretty far from your scene."

"Huh?" Arno looked almost hurt that she had said this. "You invited me. Don't you remember?"

"Oh, did I? I invited so many people," Liesel said breezily. "But I'm glad you're here."

"Anyway, I just wanted to say I'm really pissed that my friend stole your horse," Arno went on, in the same weird, earnest voice. "I just wanted to make sure you were, you know, okay. And say that I was sorry. That whole stunt Mickey pulled was really childish."

"Oh," Liesel said coyly, trying to think of what had changed about Arno since the winter, when they'd last hooked up. "Is that why you're here? It's okay. It's not your fault. And anyway, that wasn't *my* horse. I just borrowed it for the day."

"Um, so you're not upset?" Arno said. He shifted like he wasn't sure how to act anymore.

"Whatever," Liesel said. "Get over here."

Liesel was, after all, the daughter of people who had

made an art out of collecting art. And other precious objects. She didn't waste time. When Arno hesitated for a minute, she grabbed his ironic first season *American Idol* T-shirt and pulled him so that he was basically forced to push her against the wood-paneled wall of the ladies' room. He hesitated again, so she put his hands in place and started kissing him ferociously.

They made out for another ten minutes, in which Liesel remembered how much she liked making out with Arno, and also how great they looked together, which must have been why he'd made her invite list, and then she detached herself.

"We'd better go back into the party," she said forcefully, because Arno didn't seem quite ready yet. "People will start to talk."

"Yeah," Arno said, brushing his dark mop of hair into place. "Sorry."

Liesel tossed back her head and laughed, because really, sometimes the weirdest things came out of Arno's pretty mouth. "Don't be *sorry*. That was hot."

She turned and started to fix her mascara in the mirror, and then redid the buttons of her dress. When Arno didn't say anything, she went on, "You're acting different somehow, but you can't deny that you still want it. We make a steaming hot couple."

Arno shrugged and leaned his long frame against the

wall. "I'm a different person since we last, you know . . . I've been trying to change. Not be so shallow. I guess I just don't know if . . ."

Liesel didn't hear the rest of what Arno was saying, because she was laughing with her whole body now. Feelings were nice and everything, but she didn't usually have time for them. "Oh Awno," she said, when she managed to calm down. "That was a good one." She refocused in the mirror for a minute, drawing her fingers over her perfect skin to make sure it was still perfect.

Then she met Arno's dark eyes in the mirror. He was staring at her, he couldn't help it, and for a moment she just stared back. Then suddenly she remembered inviting him and realized why it had seemed so important to do so. "Wildenbuwger, you should just accept your fate now."

Arno stared back at her like he had no idea what she was talking about.

"*Me,* Awno," Liesel said, cracking a smile. "I am so totally your fate."

Then she went back to reapplying mascara.

### i meet a real-life party girl!

Once I got over the shock of seeing Jonathan's new girlfriend, and realizing that she was a totally self-serious boring kind of girl, and not at all like the exciting girl I would soon become, I started to really enjoy my brother's friend's ex-girlfriend's sweet sixteen party. I mean, a party like that is just the perfect excuse to be totally girlie and fun, and whoever Liesel was, she had totally done that. I mean, pink bows everywhere and an entrance on a white horse? So. Much. Fun.

And even though it took a minute of adjusting to my old friend Liv's whole new I'm-sexy-so-stare-at-me vibe, I soon realized that it was actually a purely good thing. Because, you know what? A friend who's confident and gorgeous is way more fun to get out on the dance floor with and just be a little crazy with and go around talking to random guys you think are cute with. Liv, as I found out, is very down for this kind of thing. Who knew?

Still, after a bunch of hours of partying, seeing Jonathan all wrapped up in that Ava chick started getting to me. I mean, they have every right to snuggle, but I just got sort of tired of watching it. So I decided to head off for the bathroom and splash some water on my face and remind myself that I was here to have a super-duper silly hot Saturday night.

Which is how I ended up in this epic bathroom line.

So I was feeling a little low, you know, standing in this line, looking out at all these people having fun and in couples and stuff, when—oh my God!—the most amazing thing happened.

I met Sara-Beth Benny. From TV.

This is how it happened: I am standing in this line, trying really hard not to look in Jonathan's direction. Even though I am not looking in his direction, I know exactly where he is and for some reason I'm not exactly sure of, this is making me feel very strangely nervous. And as I'm busy not looking in this one certain direction, somebody comes and taps me on my arm.

I look over and there is this very small girl

with a black wig and big sunglasses on and a dress made out of a material I wouldn't want to have touching my skin. I have sensitive skin, but still. So I'm confused at first, and then I remember that Liv saw this girl in big shades earlier who she was convinced was SBB. Before I can say anything, the girl in the wig hooks our elbows together, and she leans in to say something in my ear.

"I am Sara . . . Beth . . . Benny," she said in this slow, dramatic voice. "And I need to cut into line with you."

"Okay," I said. I looked back, and saw that the line had gotten really long behind me. A couple people looked annoyed by the line-cutter, but no one was going to say anything.

"Thank you *so much*," Sara-Beth went on emphatically, like she really meant it. She was tiny, like she had been magically shrunken, and her skin had this supernatural perfection to it, like it was almost translucent or something. "You are a sweet thing. I knew it just from looking at you."

"Are you okay?" I said, because it was all a little weird.

"Oh, I am so good, you don't even know, I mean just fantastic, just super," she said in a big rush of words. Then she paused, and said,

"Except that I have to, you know, be in disguise all the time."

"I was wondering why you were dressed like that," I said, trying not to sound shy, which of course I did anyway.

Sara-Beth sighed, and leaned on me with all of her weight, which didn't even feel like that much. "I'm undercover," she said in a stage whisper.

"Why?"

"Because I got a part in this film, and it's the role of a lifetime, but they're worried about my reputation."

"What reputation?" I said, like that was shocking to me, even though of course I knew exactly what she had a reputation for. *Celeb Lives* runs a story like every week about how she's always going out and getting in trouble for being so wild.

"Oh, they think I'm like this off-her-nut party girl. Whatever." She sighed again, this time like she'd heard it all before. "Anyway, so in my contract it says I can't be photographed or reported 'partying.'"

"That's awful," I said, like she'd just told me her puppy had been kidnapped.

"I know, and the worst part is that . . ." She paused, and looked around to make sure that nobody was listening. "The worst part is that this basically separates me from my soul mate, who I am so desperately in love with."

"Oh no!"

"Don't worry," Sara-Beth said, stroking my hand. "I found him." Then she smiled happily, like that explained it all. "So . . . what's your name?"

"Flannery Flood," I said, "but everybody just calls me Flan."

"Flood . . ." SBB put a finger to her temple, signaling thought. "Are you Patch Flood's little sister?"

"Uh-huh."

"Oh, that must be why you're so pretty," she said sweetly. "I've met your brother. He's been nice to me."

I just nodded, because I'm basically deaf to compliments about my brother at this point, even if they are coming from a huge star.

"And, he's friends with my soul mate," SBB continued enthusiastically.

"Really?" I said. I had been picturing a tall, dark, swaggering self-made hotelier or something. And I would definitely know if my brother knew such a person.

"Uh-huh. And he's soooo cute. Maybe you know him?" She grabbed my hand, and smiled at me like we'd been bff since second grade. "His name's David."

"David *Grobart*?" I said, squinting my eyes at her before I could make myself stop. It isn't that David isn't cute or anything—he is, and really tall—but he's sort of dopey. And he kind of had a crush on me at the same time Jonathan and I were going out, which means that Sara-Beth Benny and I have love life history in common. Which is *the weirdest.* "Really?" was all I could say.

"Really," Sara-Beth said, and her face was all bright and sunshiny. Then all of a sudden, it wasn't. "Why isn't this line moving?"

"I don't know," I said. It was odd, now that she mentioned it—we hadn't moved at all since SBB had cut in with me—but for some reason I was struck by this need to keep her from getting upset. So I said: "But isn't this sort of nice? I feel like now we've had all this time to get to know each other. "

And just like that SBB's mood changed again. She seemed to be agreeing with me, but she also seemed to be glowing from within with this molten core of vulnerability. *"Yes,"* she said, grabbing my shoulder. "It is *so* nice to just girl-talk like this, even if it is in a bathroom line, it is just so really very nice."

"Yeah," I said, nodding my head furiously. "Totally so nice . . ."

"Oh my God, you have no idea. Since I signed this contract it's like I've been in hiding and I haven't seen any of my girlfriends."

"That's awful. But can't they come over to your house?" I said.

"I've grown very afraid of my apartment," SBB nearly wailed. "And all my friends are mean, mean, mean girls."

"Oh," I said, because there's really no way to make a thing like that okay, right?

"Yeah."

"Well . . . you can come over and hang at my place if you want," I said, before I could realize that I was inviting a celebrity over to my house. "I mean, my friend Liv just got into town, and she's basically living there, so I mean, there are two of us. And it will be fun. Like a big sleepover or something!"

SBB's face was sunny again, like it had been when she was talking about David. "Really?" she said. "I can really come over for a sleepover? With you?"

"Of course," I told her.

SBB threw her arms around me and squeezed. "I *knew* I liked you!"

Over her head, I saw my brother's friend Arno walk out of the bathroom, wearing the face he probably usually reserves for when it's six a.m. and he's trying to leave an NYU dorm without the security guard seeing him. Wonder what he'd been up to . . .

## where do those boys disappear to?

*"This is Jonathan, leave a message with your number, the best time to reach you, and the latest news after the beep."* BEEP

"J., hey, it's David, sorry I disappeared from the party. I just dropped SBB off at my apartment 'cuz she was really beat, but the whole thing is just weird and kind of freaking me out. I mean, she's back, she thinks she's living here again, she wants me to be in a movie or some crazy shit . . . Um, can I come meet you? Where'd you guys end up? Call me back."

*"You've reached the number of Liesel Reid. Ciao ciao."* BEEP

"Hey Liesel, it's Philippa. It's been too long and I wanted to catch up and your party was great and it would be so cool if you got to meet my girlfriend, Stella, but she didn't feel all that well tonight, so we had to go home early. Sorry about that. But happy birthday! And let's talk. Mua!"

*"Hi, uh, this is David, leave me a um . . ." BEEP*
"David, where are you? What are you doing? It's Jonathan. We're at Lotus. Get your ass over here."

## it's all about the girlie after party

"I still cannot believe you met SBB," Liv, who was lying on her back on the big, soft flokati in the middle of Flan's bedroom floor, said. She had been saying this all night—basically since Jonathan had put them in a cab when Liesel Reid's party started winding down— but she'd quieted a bit over the last hour. It seemed like a good time to restate her position. Even in the middle of the night it was hot, and all the windows in the house were thrown open. Liv's hair was spread out all around her, and she had on the matching Cosabella camisole and boy shorts she had bought online just before she left boarding school. They made her feel very grown-up. "I can't believe you met her *without* me," she clarified.

"I know, I *know*," Flan said. Her light brown hair was in a half pulled-through ponytail on the top of her head, and she had washed her makeup off, so she was looking very shiny and fresh-faced sitting on the wicker sleigh bed that was just big enough to sleep the both of them. She was wearing this huge white sack of a night-gown. "I'm sorry! But you'll get to meet her tomorrow, when—"

"What!?" Liv twisted up off the floor and looked directly at her friend. "Shut up and tell me!"

"When SBB . . . comes to my house . . . for a sleep-over . . ."

"No!" Liv's mouth hung open. She tried to shut it and couldn't.

"Yup," Flan said. She had one of those big smiles on her face that you can't get rid of, no matter how hard you try, because what you're saying is so big and excit-ing. "She needs friends, because she's undercover, and she wants *us* to be those friends."

"Oh. My. Freakin'. Lord." Liv admitted to herself that she was impressed by Flan. At first, she hadn't really thought she'd changed all that much, but invit-ing a movie star over, that took moxie.

"You want to see her number?" Flan said, passing Liv her cell phone so that Liv could key through and see what the cell number of a TV star and notorious party girl really looked like.

"This is too exciting," Liv said. "Do you think she'll bring clothes?"

Flan shrugged kind of seriously, and said, "I don't

think so. I think she's trying to be un-starletlike, you know what I mean?"

"Mmmm . . ." Liv thought about this for a minute. It was *sort* of disappointing. But after the fun New York night she'd had, she wasn't about to let it bring her down. "You know what this means, right?"

"What?" Flan said.

"What it means is, tonight was only the beginning," Liv said, smiling knowingly at her friend.

"Beginning of what?"

"Of our summer. Of partying. I mean, I'm here one night, and already we're gonna be hanging with a real celebrity?" Liv shook her head, like it had all been told. "We're taking this town by storm."

"You think so?" Flan said.

"Oh, hon, I *know* so," Liv replied. They both fell silent for a minute, while Liv pictured all the parties she was going to go to and all the people who would want to talk to her. She could almost physically feel herself transforming into the kind of girl Patch Flood couldn't keep from falling in love with if he tried. Or even if a small army of angry parents was against it.

That was when they heard the noisy hooting of male voices from the first floor. The guys had gone to some other party after the Boat House, supposedly to look for Patch, which Liv was all for because she didn't like his whole disappearing act. How could she impress him with how hot she was now if they weren't even in the same room? But the guys were back now, and they were so loud that there pretty much had to be five of them. Liv and Flan looked at each other; somebody on the first floor was being teased. Liv couldn't help but wonder if that person was Patch, and if he was being teased about some gigantic crush . . . which he had just admitted to having . . . on her?

"Flan," Liv said, crawling toward her innocently on her elbows, "let's go down there. And party with them."

"I dunno," Flan said slowly.

"Why not?"

"Well, it's just . . ."

"*C'mon*, you get to hang out with those guys all the time," Liv said, her voice rising. She could feel an opportunity to flirt with Patch slipping away from her, and she didn't like it. "Don't be selfish."

"I'm not being selfish," Flan said defensively, "and it's not like I hang out with those guys all the time. And . . . there's something else."

"What?"

"You know that guy Jonathan, my brother's friend? The one with the beautiful, soft leather motorcycle jacket?"

"Yeah?"

"He's my ex."

"Really?" Liv knew she was supposed to be sympathetic right now—Flan had just told her that she'd spent all night hanging around her ex and his new girlfriend—but she also found this news kind of exciting. "Wow . . . he's cute."

"I know, but . . . *you* know."

"I know," Liv said. "But you know what? This gives us even more reason to go down and hang out. Because you know why? It will show that you weren't bothered by him having his new . . . friend there tonight."

"You think?"

"Definitely," Liv said, punctuating her words with a head bob. She walked over to the mirror on the back of Flan's door and fussed with her hair. "And then maybe he'll start wondering if that new friend is the right special friend in the first place."

**it's so not about straining to hang out with oblivious older dudes . . . or is it?**

When they got downstairs, Liv and Flan saw that the guys had all been sitting on the oatmeal-colored couches and love seats in the living room. They were all semi-reclined, with their arms thrown back against the upholstery, and they had the appearance of people who had been many places and seen many things. They stood up as soon as they saw the girls, in an awkward show of gentlemanly behavior, and said hi in unison.

Liv felt her heart sink when she counted only four hot older guys in the room.

"Oh, hey Flan," Patch said as he came through the door to the kitchen. He had a six-pack of tallboys dangling from his index finger, and Liv could see the broad curve of his shoulders under his rumpled oxford shirt. He nodded in Liv's direction, and said hi to her, too; when she heard him say her name it was like her whole body was on a roller coaster heading down. He said her name like it was his favorite word in the English language.

Liv tried to sound nonchalant as she said, "So, where have you guys been?"

"Lotus," David said, his eyes meeting Liv's.

"Yeah, wasn't much happening there tonight," Jonathan said. He shrugged in this way that made Liv feel like she would have given pretty much anything to have been at Lotus that night. "Lots of people, but they were all kind of lame."

Flan was just standing there awkwardly, so Liv smiled big and said, "Can we sit down?"

"Yeah, totally," David said, rearranging himself on the love seat to make room. Flan went and sat next to him, and Liv waited until Patch had taken a seat, and then she went and sat on the floor leaning against the couch he was sitting on. Everybody else resumed their sprawled, post-party position on the couches, and after a moment of silence, the guys picked up their conversation as though nothing had changed.

"Yeah," Mickey said, putting his white-clogged feet on the rusted metal-topped coffee table his father, the sculptor Ricardo Pardo, had given the Floods for their twenty-fifth wedding anniversary, "she's totally awesome. I mean, it's like somebody said let's re-create Mickey Pardo as a chick. That's pretty much what Sonya is like."

Jonathan made a noise. "Is that a good thing?"

"You mean, dating the girl version of you?" Arno said. A contemplative look came over his face, and then he jerked upward and headed for the bathroom. Mickey watched Arno leave, and then chugged his beer.

"What about you, Jonathan?" Liv said. She winked at Flan, whose teeth were visibly clenched. "What's up with your girlfriend?'

Jonathan didn't say anything for a long moment, as though he were trying to determine the level of his drunkenness or who the word "girlfriend" referred to in this context. "Ava?" he said finally, but his eyebrows were still scrunched together. "Oh . . . yeah . . . she's making raw food soups to sell at her school Monday. She's going to donate the profits to some animal shelter in Brooklyn. I'm supposed to help. At nine."

Everyone stared at him in silence.

"So, yeah, I guess I should be going," Jonathan said, standing up and wrapping himself in his motorcycle jacket. He stumbled toward the door, looking a lot more drunk than he had when he was sitting down. When he reached the arched entryway to the foyer, he paused and said, "I never realized how early nine in the morning is."

"I think our friend Jonathan has had one too many," Mickey said, standing and stumbling into the coffee table, "which is a thing I know all about. I'm going to go find him a cab." And then Mickey disappeared in the direction Jonathan had gone, somehow making a lot more noise in the process.

"The pink champagne will do it." Patch chuckled in David's direction. An adorable smile flashed across his face.

"I'm fine," David said quickly.

"What? I know *you're* fine," Patch said, twisting his head slightly and squinting at David. He paused, and then stood. "I think it's time for me to hit the hay."

"Oh, okay," David said. "Can I just finish my beer?"

"Yeah, whatever," Patch said. "Good night."

Liv stood up and yawned dramatically. "I think I've got to go to bed, too." Flan looked like she might get up and follow her, so Liv made her eyes all saucerlike until her friend sat still. "Nighty-night."

She winked at Flan and David, who were now sitting awkwardly on a love seat by themselves. Liv didn't really think they would kiss or anything, but if they did, maybe *that* would make Jonathan jealous. And Liv had already decided that her friend should totally go out with Jonathan. Or get back together with him, or whatever.

But she stopped thinking about that pretty quickly, because now she was following Patch Flood up the stairs toward all the bedrooms on the third floor. She let one of the straps of her camisole fall for good measure. Maybe Flan wasn't going to get with her guy tonight, but Liv was pretty sure that she was.

When she got to the top of the stairs, she saw that Patch was standing there with one of his shoulders resting against the wall. Was he . . . waiting for her?

"Patch?" she whispered.

He turned around. "Oh, hi Liv," he said.

His face was sort of moody, or something, so Liv said, "Are you okay?"

"Everybody always just rushes into these things, you know?" he said, his greenish eyes focused on the floor. "I can't believe David is being so flaky with SBB, who is sort of weird, I guess, but she just worships him. Everybody always has all these good intentions, and then their big love goes to shit so quickly."

Liv couldn't believe it. She almost couldn't breathe. This was better then hooking up with Patch Flood— he had basically just told her he was *so* into her that he wanted to take it slow. She stepped forward and looked into his eyes. "I totally get where you're coming from," she said simply, and then she kissed him on the cheek.

Patch looked surprised for a minute, and as Liv turned back toward Flan's room she wondered if she hadn't taken it too far. But by the time she was curled up in her half of the sleigh bed, reimagining all the amazing things that had happened to her tonight, she had decided it was just the right gesture. It definitely said: "I also think we should take it slow, but I am so totally into you, too."

Liv smiled to herself as she fell asleep.

## philippa has excellent taste

"This is sort of my special little place," Stella said, shrugging proudly at Philippa and Mickey and Sonya. She obviously thought Bar d'O, the drag queen place in the West Village that she took them to on Sunday night, was a very big deal. "Can we have that table near the window?" she asked the hostess, who was channeling Madonna in her nouveau-disco-queen phase. As the hostess led them to that table, Stella turned and said, "That's just my special little table."

Philippa, who was wearing a black Prada cocktail dress that used to be her mother's and Converse, couldn't help but notice that Mickey and Sonya, with whom she and Stella were on their second double date, were eye-laughing with each other. Then she saw Sonya mouth *jackass* at Mickey.

When they sat down, Stella took out her wallet and said, "I'm buying. Mickey, you're Cuban, right? They make great mojitos here. Four mojitos." She turned and strode to the bar.

Mickey and Sonya couldn't help but giggle at all this, and Philippa felt herself joining in. "What a Jonathan, huh?" she said.

"Total Jonathan," Mickey said, nodding.

"Who's Jonathan?" Sonya asked.

"One of my oldest friends," Mickey said. "He's really into knowing what's hot and, you know, being able to get in hot places. And then, once he's in there, knowing what's hot to drink."

Philippa nodded and smiled in agreement. It was weird how good it felt, having someone she and Mickey knew in common who Sonya was clueless about. Besides, Philippa had always liked Jonathan, and she had faith that he would keep Mickey in line now that she wasn't around to do it anymore. Then she remembered that this had all started because Mickey and Sonya were making fun of her girlfriend. "I just think Stella felt sort of out of her element last night," Philippa said defensively, "you know, with the sweet sixteen and everything. So she wants to show us her spots tonight. I guess that's why she's acting . . . like a jackass. Kind of."

Sonya nodded like she still thought it was pretty funny, and then she leaned over to whisper something in Mickey's ear. Sonya was wearing a sparkly halter top and skinny-ankle jeans.

"So," Philippa said, trying to get back in the conversation, "what did you guys do all day?"

"Wow," Sonya said, laughing and pushing her long hair back off her shoulder. "Just hung out, I guess. Breakfast at Veselka, we went to that Japanese place on Ninth Street that has all those vintage T-shirts and shit . . ." Mickey pointed to the Mickey Mouse shirt he was wearing. "I don't know," Sonya went on, "nothing much."

"Um, nothing much?" Mickey said sarcastically.

"What? What am I forgetting?"

"Brooklyn Bridge?" Mickey was widening his big eyes at Sonya like a wounded boyfriend. "The orange Vespa?"

"Oh, right!" Sonya slapped her hand down on the table. "We went to the Vespa dealers on Crosby and test-drove a scooter."

"Across the Brooklyn Bridge," Mickey added excitedly in Philippa's direction.

"The pedestrian pathway of the Brooklyn Bridge, actually," Sonya put in, "which was *hilarious.*"

"Everyone was screaming—"

"—jumping out of the way, 'you morons!' You know, like that—"

Philippa found herself nodding along excitedly with

their story, even though they were totally wrapped up in each other. But how could she not nod along? This used to be her story.

"And eventually this cop pulls us over and is like threatening to arrest us . . ." Mickey said, rolling his eyes.

"Oh no," Philippa said, involuntarily putting her hands over her mouth. She hated when cops entered Mickey's stories.

"Don't be such a ninny," Sonya said. "It all worked out fine, because I just suddenly really wanted to kiss Mickey, right there on the pedestrian walkway of the Brooklyn Bridge, with, you know, those beautiful spans overhead and the sea breeze and all the people yelling at us and—"

"And the cop, don't forget the cop. He thought we were cute, so he let us go," Mickey concluded.

"How romantic," Stella said, coughing her hoarse smoker's cough. She was standing by their table with four green drinks.

"Oh, hi," Philippa said, glad to see her girlfriend after listening to Sonya and Mickey's kissing story. She reached over to her for a kiss, but Stella didn't move any closer, and the whole thing came off awkwardly. There was a moment of silence, and then everyone slurped their mojitos.

"I just love drag, and how it, like, turns gender on

its head . . ." Stella was saying. The night had progressed considerably, and it was now late enough that she was smoking in the bar. Out in the middle of the floor, a heavy and diaphanous drag queen was telling raunchy jokes.

Mickey was several mojitos in, and slumped against the back of the booth, but he still managed to look bored by this latest pseudo-academic nugget from his ex-girlfriend's new girlfriend.

"I mean, you think about how this challenges all of our socially constructed preconceptions about—"

"Yawn," Mickey said. "Hey, where's Sonya?"

Philippa put her arm around Stella, to reassure her that *she* didn't think the lecture was boring, but Stella hadn't seemed to take offense anyway. "I don't know," she said. "Maybe she realized she was a lesbian after all, and ran off with a—"

"Oh, there she is," Mickey interrupted. They all looked up and saw Sonya bellied up to the glowing orange bar. Next to her was the disco Madonna, and they appeared to be in the middle of a tequila shooting competition. The bartender would pour them a shot, and they would knock it back. Rinse, repeat.

"Holy cow," Mickey said, his face filling up with admiration.

"I'm not sure this is a good thing," Philippa said.

"Definitely not a good thing," Stella put in.

"Come on! You drink like a little boy!" Sonya yelled at the Madonna, who was looking a little queasy and pulling at his wig.

"Oh dear," Stella said.

The Madonna looked around the room to see if anyone was watching. Several regulars were.

"If you can't handle the heat, why don't you just crown *me* queen," Sonya yelled tauntingly. The little group that had formed around them thought that was pretty funny, and clapped, so the Madonna reluctantly nodded at the bartender to pour them two more shots.

Philippa watched in horror as Sonya lifted her shot glass, said, "Who's the big queen now?!" and knocked hers back. The Madonna shot his as well, and immediately fell backward onto the floor. Upon impact, he projectile vomited.

"Holy herd of cows!" Mickey yelled, standing up excitedly.

"What the fuck?" the drag queen in the middle of the room said. He stopped his routine and looked from the fallen Madonna to Sonya and back again. Sonya looked like she was trying not to laugh. Finally the drag queen said, "What in hell did you do to Richard? Get out of here, you little *hussy.*"

Suddenly the lights went up, and a lot of mean-looking drag queens were staring Sonya down.

"We gotta get out of here," Philippa said.

"Good idea," Stella said.

Mickey ran up and grabbed Sonya by the hand and pulled her out of the bar with Philippa and Stella close behind.

Much later, when Stella had gone home to study for her summer class, Philippa found herself on another bridge with Sonya and Mickey. They were more or less at the bottom of a fifth of Cuervo and a hint of the sun was making their view of the East River all golden, from the point where it flowed out from under the Williamsburg Bridge.

At some point Philippa had gotten tired of hearing about how much fun Sonya and Mickey thought each other were, so she started talking about her relationship. She hadn't been able to stop.

"She's so smart and cool and I just"—Philippa knew she sounded drunk, but she kept on with it—"*love* her soooo much."

"You do not," Sonya said sharply, but with a smile. She was pressing her abdomen against the metal railing of the bridge, and leaning into the dewy, salty air. "Love her, I mean."

Philippa knew, even in her tequila-fogged state, that Sonya was telling the truth. And she hated her for it.

**all sbb wants is a normal life, like any normal
girl, except with nicer clothes**

After a Grobart family Monday night dinner of
thin-crust veggie pizza and grape juice spritzers, Sara-
Beth Benny—who had moved back in to the Grobarts'
West Village apartment after reconnecting with their
son Saturday night—pulled David into his room and
wrapped her arms around his neck.

"Your mom seems so happy," she said, smiling up
at him.

"My mom?" David said. "Um, why?"

"Oh, you know," SBB said, inhaling the nice, clean-
but-still-a-little-sweaty smell David always had after
basketball practice and a shower. She loved that smell. It
smelled like real guy, as opposed to all those overly man-
icured boys she knew in the TV business. "Because the
family is back together . . . I just think she seemed so at
peace tonight, having all of us around her."

"I don't think Mom . . . ," David started. "Um, never mind. I'm sure you're right."

"I know I'm right," SBB said, grabbing at David's T-shirt, "which is why I'm so afraid."

"Afraid of what?"

"Well"—SBB opened her blue eyes at David—"I need some girl time."

"Girl time?"

"Yeah, with my new friends. Flan and Lynn."

"Lynn?" David said, twisting a little bit so that SBB had to let go of his shirt. "You mean Liv?"

"Right, Liv," SBB said. "Oh, you're annoyed, aren't you? But listen, because I can't see any of my old friends, I really need to spend some time with my new girlfriends. Is that okay with you and Mom? I mean, you and Hilary?"

"Yeah," David said, "sure, that's cool. Go hang with Liv. And Flan. Flan and Liv."

"Okay," SBB said. "Are you sure? It's really okay if . . ."

"No, go . . . go . . . ," David said, taking SBB's two small hands in his, squeezing them, and then letting them go.

"Oh no!" she wailed, covering her face with her hands. "You *are* mad!"

"No, no, no!" David waved at her, like he was trying to direct traffic in a snowstorm. "Not mad, not mad!"

She peeked through her fingers. "Really?"

"No! I mean, yes! Please, go, have fun. I'm okay. Really."

A smile broke out over Sara-Beth's face, and she threw her arms around David again, this time at his middle. "David, you are such . . . a good . . . *mmmph* . . . guy."

"Thanks," David said, petting her head. "I'm going to go catch the beginning of the Yankees game on TV, okay? Say bye when you leave?"

"Okay." Sara-Beth beamed a smile up at David—good, understanding David.

"Oh, and by the way, I might come by Patch's later. Might not happen, but Arno and I were talking about going over there tonight. But don't worry, I know not to crowd," David said, taking a deep breath. "You won't even know I'm there."

Sara-Beth threw on a low-key Barneys black knit poncho over tight black leggings, and then put her black wig back on. She waved good-bye to the Grobarts, who looked like the light was about to go out of their lives—sometimes, she felt like they needed her as much as she needed them, but only sometimes. Then she hurried down to her waiting limo. On the way to Flan's house, she made the driver pull over for a bottle of Baileys and three packages of tamari-flavored rice crisps.

When SBB got to the Floods', she was greeted on the steps by her two new younger girlfriends.

"Hi!" Flan said, jumping up and kissing SBB on either cheek.

"Hello, sweetie," SBB said. "You look just gorgeous."

"Thanks," Flan said, brushing her brownish hair over her ear and looking sort of embarrassed by the compliment. She ducked her head when she talked, which SBB knew from her movement class signified humility. "This is my friend Liv, who I told you about."

Liv extended her hand forcefully. "It's such an honor," she said. "I mean, your spread in *W*? The Mumbai look? My total fashion inspiration for all of second-semester eighth grade!"

"That's nice of you to say," SBB said, lowering her voice and looking around to make sure nobody on Perry Street was watching. "But I'm really not here to be my celebrity self. This is just me, okay?"

"Okay," Flan said, ushering her into the house and then up the stairs. "We made cookies, too, so you can feel really normal!"

SBB felt her heart clutch a little. "Oh . . . thanks. You girls are terrible, though! I have to be camera-ready in like under two weeks!"

"Oh, that's okay!" Flan said quickly.

"Yeah, we can just donate them to homeless people or something," Liv added.

"I brought rice crisps," SBB added hopefully as they came off the third-floor landing into Flan's room, which was all normal and covered with pillows and fashion mags. "Oh my God, this is perfect!" SBB said, throwing herself into the big comfy sleigh bed in the middle of the room. Then she noticed the collage of pictures of Leland Brinker on the wall behind the bed, most of them from the album sleeve of his debut album, *Peppermint Girls on the Brink*.

Sara-Beth raised her eyebrows at Flan. "Leland Brinker, huh?"

"Who's Leland Brinker?" Liv asked.

"Oh, you know," Flan said bashfully, "he's that folk protégé. He's like eighteen but he sounds like Bob Dylan and hangs out with Norah Jones and people like that."

"I hooked up with him, you know," Sara-Beth said, sitting up. "Leland, I mean."

"You know that's been there forever," Flan said, suddenly even more embarrassed by her bedroom wall collage. "I really meant to take it down by now."

"Don't be embarrassed, he's hot!" Sara-Beth said impulsively. For some reason, she felt a strong urge to make Flan feel okay about everything. "But not as hot as David," she added.

Liv and Flan came and sat gingerly on the bed. "How long have you been with David?" Liv asked. "If you don't mind my asking."

"Oh my God, not long at all, but it's like so . . ." Sara-Beth felt all warm inside at the mention of David, and her eyes glazed over as she tried to think of some good way of describing him. "He's just right," she said, "that's all."

"Yeah," Liv said dreamily. "I know what you mean."

"Did you have fun on Saturday night?" Flan asked.

"I thought it was a great party," SBB said. "I mean, I've been to so many parties in the last year that they all blur, but that one was special. Because Liesel is special to me. We knew each other when we were little girls. Did you have a good time?"

"Oh my God!" Flan clasped her hands together and looked up at the ceiling. "Such a good time! I loved everything about it. The horse and the place and all those flowers and—"

"Now Flan wants her own sweet sixteen," Liv gushed. SBB could always tell when people wanted to talk to her so badly that they would be unable to do anything but just say whatever came into their heads. Liv was one of those people, but SBB resolved not to let it reflect on Flan. After all, SBB completely understood that you could be a terrific person and still end up being surrounded by other people who could be, well, not so great.

"You know what—you should *have* a sweet sixteen!" SBB said, beaming at Flan. "Why not? That would be so much fun!" Liv and Flan stared at her like they didn't know what to say. Sara-Beth, who had hated silence since she was a child, felt the need to add, "No, really, why not?"

Flan scrunched her forehead. "Because I'm only turning fourteen on Friday?" She put her hands up in the air, like she was just taking a shot at a teacher's really hard question.

"Wait—your birthday is *this* Friday?" Sara-Beth brought herself up on her knees on the bed and reached for Flan's shoulders with both hands. "Don't wait, sweetie. If you want a sweet sixteen party, don't listen to small-minded conventional people! You've got to live your dream *now*!"

## liv only overhears good news

"I'm just going to go get a glass of water, okay?" Liv said, standing up and moving away from the bed. Flan and SBB looked at her like she was a person whose name they couldn't quite remember. They were both wearing dunky pajamas that Flan had found in the bottom of her drawer.

"Oh, will you get me some?" Sara-Beth said.

"Sure," Liv said as she hurried out of the bedroom and down the stairs. She'd been annoyed for a minute, because her friends just kept talking about themselves, but as soon as she was down in the big, airy kitchen with its industrial table and virtually unused Viking range, she felt all that slipping away. It was like her mother had always told her: Groups of three are tough. And it wasn't like her old friend Flan and her new friend SBB were being *mean*. No, Liv decided as she got a bottle of Evian out of the fridge and took a sip, definitely not mean. It was just that they were really excited about their things—in Flan's case, her possible sweet sixteen party, and in SBB's, her weirdly normal-guy boyfriend, David.

And that was fine for them. Liv's thing—the beginning of her relationship with Patch—was not something that she really felt comfortable talking about yet, since they'd agreed on Saturday night that they really had to take it slow.

"I just don't know if I'm into long-distance relationships," a voice was saying.

Liv froze, nearly choking up her Evian. She knew that voice—ever so slightly nasally, slow, nonchalant—and it made her feel all giddy and sexy and *wanted.*

"Yeah, they're a total bitch," said another voice. Different, and less recognizable, but still not an entirely unfamiliar voice. Sort of blasé: that pretty boy Arno, definitely.

The voices were moving through the hall, past the kitchen, and into the living room. Liv moved toward the kitchen doorway, trying to hear better. She *needed* to hear better, because one of those voices was Patch's, and he was speaking to a topic that concerned her a lot. The concept of a long-distance relationship had been weighing on her mind ever since Saturday night, when Patch had first told her that he wanted to take it slow. Because even though she wasn't acting like it, she was supposed to be in Cambridge, England, right now for the orientation of her pre–high school academic program. And she wasn't going to be able to play hooky forever, which would mean that taking it slow would lead to a *very* long-distance relationship.

A transatlantic love affair.

"I just really screwed up, relationship-wise, you know what I mean," the voice she was pretty sure belonged to Arno said. "That whole thing with Lara— I thought she was what I wanted and by the time I figured out that what I actually wanted was something totally different, I'd already screwed that up."

Liv was tempted to push through the door and point out that what Arno was saying was not in any way related to Patch's feelings for her, but she was saved from doing so when the sexy voice started up again.

"I'm not sure if that's exactly what I was talking about, man," Patch said. "But I'm sorry things got messed up with that girl."

"Thanks, dude."

"Anyway, I just feel like . . ."

Liv leaned against the door. She was pretty sure that Patch was still saying something, but they'd turned on the TV, and she couldn't hear anything over it. She was pretty sure she heard him say "love of my life," although that also could have been whatever movie they were watching.

There were a few moments of silence, during which Liv could feel her heart pounding against her Cosabella camisole. Then a voice that was definitely Arno's said, "Well, dude, I'm no expert on love. But I wouldn't rule anything out just 'cuz of geography."

Liv gasped "Right on!" out loud, and drew her clenched fist backward in a *yes!* motion. She couldn't help it, he was just so *right.* Then she remembered that Patch didn't know that she was hiding in the kitchen, and that maybe if he found her there, he would think that she wasn't taking the whole "take it slow" thing seriously. She grabbed her Evian and hurried to the other kitchen door—the one that led straight into the hall.

She was looking behind her as she reached for the door and stepped out of the kitchen, just to make sure that Patch wasn't coming to see what the noise had been, and that's when she ran right into him.

Liv stood there in the hall, her face pressed into a chest that was so strong, and good smelling—a little bit clean, a little bit dirty—that it could only have belonged to Patch. After all, only someone as superhumanly hot as Patch could have gotten from the living room to the hall that quickly. For a moment, they both stood still, savoring the moment. She kept her eyes closed, and decided to feel him out the way blind people do, with her hands. First she felt his shoulders, and then his chin, and then she stood on her tiptoes and kissed him.

It was like little darts of pure ecstasy were hitting her all over. She wanted to look into his eyes immediately, but she tried to resist.

Slowly, slowly she pulled her lips away and opened her eyes, and when she did, she realized she'd made a mistake.

"Um, this isn't right," David said, pulling away from her.

"I *know*," Liv wailed, trying to keep her voice down. Patch was still out there in the living room and, of course, David's girlfriend, who was also Liv's style icon, was only two flights up. "How could you?" she said.

"I didn't mean . . ." David stammered.

"Never mind," Liv said, and without taking another look at David she went huffing up the stairs, and back to Flan's bedroom, where, luckily, there were no boys allowed tonight.

**for liesel reid, work and social life
are like the same thing**

"Hotel Gansevoort," Liesel said, sliding into the cab and nearly dumping the contents of her mandarin Via Spiga tote all over the backseat. "You should take Hudson."

As soon as the cab pulled away from the corner of Mercer and Broome, where DeeDee Rakoff's public relations firm was located, Liesel grabbed her cell phone and called her drinks date, Sara-Beth Benny.

"Hello, darling! It's me, Lies," she said, once SBB had picked up. "I'm on my way and I just wanted to let you know that I'm running about fifteen minutes behind sched—what? You know I basically had to sign over my trust fund to get a reservation at the Hotel Gansevoort . . . I understand . . . Gotcha, gotcha . . . See you in ten . . . Ciao, ciao." Liesel snapped her phone shut and dropped it back in her bag. "Change of plans, we ah going to Cowgirl on the corner of Hudson and West Tenth, okay? You can still take Hudson."

Liesel found SBB in the back room of the Cowgirl Hall of Fame, which was decorated with cow skulls and kitsch western paintings and seemed, especially on a warm summer evening, very dark and cavelike. SBB was hiding behind a strawberry frozen margarita in an oversized glass mug, and she was wearing a belted trench over black leggings and white flats. When she saw Liesel, she pushed her wig back to get a better look. "Baby!"

Liesel kissed her on either cheek and then sat down next to her. "This is . . . *private*, but you know the Hotel Gansevoort has a bar on the roof with fabulous people and delicious dwinks. You could actually get some air, gorgeous."

Liesel hoped that didn't come out all mothering and concerned, which was of course also how she had meant it. She had known SBB since before *Mike's Princesses*, and she never liked to see her friend hiding in a role. Or big sunglasses.

"I know." SBB made a pouting/apologetic face. "I'm sorry. I just can't be photographed, especially not in a bar, and that place is full of gossip people. I'm sorry."

"Ugh, it's fine, darling, but really, who's repping you? Clearly they don't know the first rule of PR: All news is good news." Liesel leaned back against the low desert-modern couch and crossed her long, almost boyishly thin legs. She was wearing what had basically become her work uniform since she started interning at DeeDee Rakoff during the fall semester: a houndstooth blazer with the collar turned up, black capri pants, and a white blouse. It made her feel very businesslike, even when she knew it was time to turn the businesslike off. "SBB, I'm so glad we managed to fit this in. Such a treat!"

"I know," SBB said and clasped Leisel's hand, just as the waitress appeared. SBB instinctively pulled at her wig, so that strands of black hair fell across her cheekbones, and Liesel, still holding her hand, leaned forward and ordered a strawberry margarita.

"Are you over twenty-one?" the waitress asked. She said it in a demanding way, but Liesel could tell she didn't really want to ask.

Liesel smiled confidently. "Twenty-two, actually." She made a motion like she was reaching for her wallet. "Do you want to see my ID?" she asked in a voice that implied that that would just waste both of their time.

"No, that's okay," the waitress said. "I trust you. You want a refill?" she added in SBB's direction, and SBB nodded.

When the waitress was gone, SBB turned to Liesel and said, "Being carded is so refreshing."

"I know! Ever since I've signed up with DeeDee, it's

like no one even questions me anymore. Which is understandable on the one hand, and creepy on the other."

SBB nodded in agreement.

"So, did you see Philippa at the party?" Liesel went on.

"Philippa Frady?" SBB said. "From elementary school? No . . . she was there? That sucks . . . I would have liked to see her again."

"Yeah, and get this . . . she's a lesbian now."

"No!"

"Yes."

"Wow . . . huh," SBB said with a shrug. "Well, it was bound to happen. Her parents are so square. She must have a really deep psychic need to do crazy rebellious things that make her parents unhappy."

Liesel laughed throatily. "Yes, well, don't we all."

"So *anyway*, tell me about this job," SBB said, grabbing for Liesel's hand again. "I hear DeeDee is a total freak."

"She's an amazing businesswoman and I admire her tons," Liesel said, switching into her tone of official enthusiasm. "She's a total control freak, and you know, there was that whole throwing her Blackberry at her assistant thing. *Entre nous*, that girl got a settlement she so did not deserve. But I love the job. You get to talk to *everybody*, and for once"—Liesel took her margarita from the waitress, who disappeared again once she had delivered their drinks—"people admire me for being a loud-mouthed bitch."

"Hmmm . . ." SBB cocked her head and thoughtfully sucked the last chunks of frozen margarita out of the bottom of her glass. "Should I switch to DeeDee's firm?"

"Oh my God, *yes*," Liesel said. "Let me talk to some people. But that would just be fantastic, and we could totally redo your image . . ."

"I was thinking maybe like Sienna Miller? That's kind of the direction I'd like to go in . . . ," SBB said, touching the corners of her sunglasses as though she were imagining herself on the red carpet.

"We *love* Sienna," Liesel said, rolling her eyes back for emphasis. "Just love her. But you could be bigger."

"I think this next role could really send me in that direction," SBB said excitedly. "I can't really tell you anything about it, because of my contract, but it's a Ric Rodrickson project and it's filming in Gdańsk and it's going to be totally, you know, arty . . ."

"Vunderful," Liesel said, and they clinked glasses. "I just think this is going to be majuh. You, me, DeeDee . . ."

"So what's it like?" SBB got a mystical look in her eyes, like she was imagining herself in the role of junior PR girl on the make. "What are you working on?"

Liesel rolled her eyes. "There's something happening every minute in PR, you see what I mean? It's

91

exhausting. But right now I'm working on building buzz for this club called Candy—maybe you've heard of it? Opening night is this Friday."

SBB shook her head.

"It's a club for fabulous underage people, high school students who go to private schools, vacation in the Hamptons, and are on the fast track to Ivy League schools, mostly. They like to have fun, but they're not assed out."

"Wait, it's *officially* for underage people?" SBB frowned. "So they can't serve drinks? Like, how is that a party?"

"I know, these people . . . ," Liesel said, not trying to hide her disgust. "No *real* drinks, anyway. They have some featured drinks like Break on Through, the energy drink, that kind of thing. And they give away candy bracelets."

SBB's mouth was fixed in a little O of shock. "How are you ever going to make a club with no drinks hot?"

"You see what I mean? It's a challenge." Liesel shrugged. "But I'll figure something out. I always do."

"Wait! I have an idea," SBB said, putting down her drink and reaching for Liesel's hands again. "Tell me if this is, like, a good PR idea." She met Liesel's eyes, and took a deep breath. "So here's my pitch. I met this adorable eighth grader named Flan Flood, at your party the other night—"

"Wait, is she related to *Patch* Flood?"

"Yes."

"I love it already."

SBB straightened up, like she was a business girl intern, too. "So, she was totally in love with your party. *She* wants a sweet sixteen—because she's fresh-faced and excited about pure girlie fun. She's fourteen, so she's not jaded yet. She's just like the Candy girl you described. You should totally throw a Candy sweet sixteen party, to promote the club and show what it's all about. To give it personality." SBB finished with a little clap for herself and her idea.

Liesel slammed her jug of margarita down on the table, and put her hands on SBB's shoulders. "A sweet sixteen for a fourteen-year-old? Brilliant," she yelled, loud enough for the whole restaurant to hear. "I love it so much, I'm going to *make it happen.*"

## sbb can't stop the ideas

*"This is Liesel Reid at DDR PR. Leave a thorough message and I'll get back to you as soon as my schedule permits."*

"Lies, it's SBB again. It was so good to see you, and we didn't even get to talk about our boys. Next time we should get Philippa to come. But, I had this other idea I wanted to shoot your way. When I was at Flan's on Monday night, I noticed she has this homage to Leland Brinker—you know, the eighteen-year-old folk sensation who I dated once? Yeah, anyway, she has a crush on him, so maybe it would be cute if you got him to show up, like her surprise birthday date. What do you think? And, he has the same publicist as me, Vinky Morningside. Ciao, ciao."

*"Leave a message."*

"SBB, is this your phone? I hope so. Anyway, Leland Brinker! I love. I'll call Vinky."

## love hurts when you love girls

Philippa took a sip of her v and t, and gave her girl-friend, Stella, a lonesome look. Or a look that she hoped conveyed lonesomeness. Stella apparently had not gotten the point, because she was still up there singing karaoke along with Prince. Even though she sounded all screechy, everyone was cheering her along. When the song finally ended, Stella strode through the crowd kissing old friends (maybe old girlfriends?) and generally taking the long way back to the booth where Philippa was sitting all by herself.

They were in Saints, the gay bar near Stella's school, late on a Tuesday night, and pretty far from Philippa's scene. She looked around at all the strange faces, and decided that she might as well have been in Alaska.

"What a rush!" Stella said, lighting a cigarette as she sat down. Her hair was slicked back into a little bun in a way that made her features seem especially dramatic and the circles under her eyes especially dark.

"Yeah, you looked like you were having fun," Philippa said, trying to muster enthusiasm.

"Mmmm, yeah, you should do it, you look hot to-night," Stella said, draining the rest of her Budweiser.

Philippa looked down at her outfit, a Britney Spears shirt her aunt had given her when she was nine and which she hadn't thought about until Stella pulled it out and told her she thought it was awesome, and a pair of hip-hugging flared jeans. When she'd put the outfit together, she'd been trying for sexy/funny, a wink to all this collegiate irony that Stella was about, but now she just felt silly. Her mother would have called it tacky, although thankfully she hadn't seen the outfit. It wasn't Philippa's scene, and it wasn't her look, either. "Yeah, I don't really do that," Philippa said eventually. "It's against my upbringing, I guess."

"Whatever," Stella said as she blew air kisses at some butch girls over by the pool table.

"Hey, why didn't you introduce me to any of your friends?" Philippa said, and as soon as it was out of her mouth she realized that it sounded like she was trying to pick a fight. But she wasn't. Really.

"Oh . . . I will, someday. But right now they'll just ask you how recently you started dating girls. And when you tell them, they'll laugh."

"Oh," Philippa said. Her glass was empty, but she didn't really want more. "Well . . . I was thinking tomorrow night, maybe we could go see a movie with Mickey and Sonya? That would be fun, right?"

Stella sighed and stretched back into the booth. "Not really."

"You don't really want to? Or it wouldn't really be fun?"

Stella shrugged. "Both, I guess."

"Oh." Philippa twirled her empty glass and watched as her first lesbian girlfriend shifted and refused to meet her eyes. Just the way a guy would do it.

"Listen, Phil, the thing is . . . ," Stella began, jerking uncomfortably and twisting her head in a way that made the whole thing extra painful. "I'm a Barnard junior. I should be dating thirty-five-year-old women who, like, trade foreign currency and own boutique wine shops and renovate brownstones. I don't want to be hanging around with a bunch of teenagers when I go out." She made a face like she had just found a hair in her dinner. "That's just not me."

Philippa felt like she had just been hailed on, and the stinging feeling wouldn't go away. "We don't *have* to go out with Mickey and Sonya tomorrow night," she said in a very small voice. She wasn't quite sure why she was arguing, but it just felt wrong, being dumped so far away from your turf.

Stella stared at her coldly.

Philippa shook out her hair and gave her jeans a pull

upward, and then she collected her things and stood up. "Good-bye Stella," she said with what she hoped was dignity, and then she walked to the door.

When she got there, a slender boy in a cutoff T-shirt who was apparently working security that night, gave her a death glare. "What did you do to Stella?" he asked.

Philippa turned to see what she could possibly have done to Stella, and saw her now definitely ex-girlfriend sobbing dramatically and surrounded by friends. Philippa rolled her eyes. "Oh, give it a rest," she said, and then she walked out into the hot, slightly ripe-smelling Amsterdam Avenue night, and hailed a cab.

She watched buildings go by, and thought about who her friends were, and then she started to cry. Big rivers of tears that she couldn't keep from coming. Luckily, the driver was busy yelling into his mouth-piece, so Philippa had it out in the backseat and when she was done she was closer to a part of town that made some kind of sense. And by then, the only thing she wanted in the whole world was to talk to her best friend.

Mickey.

"Hey, buhbay," Mickey said, when he picked up on the fifth ring.

"Who do you think you are, Elvis?" Philippa said in a voice that couldn't hide the recent tears.

"You okay?" Mickey said.

"Are you . . . in the middle of something?"

"No."

"Oh." Philippa took a deep breath and willed herself to say it without crying: "Stella and I broke up."

"Yeah, girls are mean," Mickey said. "And mean people suck."

"No, she could be really great, she just—"

"Hey, shut it, she sucked," Mickey said. "Sorry, but it's true. Now that she's gone, you want to come over?"

"Really?"

"Hell, yeah," Mickey said. "Just watching *Braveheart* and doing a shot whenever someone loses a limb."

Philippa giggled. "That sounds like fun. Wait, you're doing this by yourself?"

"No, stupid. I'm with Sonya."

Oh, right, *her*. Philippa mouthed a very bad word to herself three times, and then she told Mickey she'd be right over. "And Mickey?" she added. "Save me some tequila, 'kay?"

**from:** liesel@ddrpr.com
**to:** vinky.morningside@vm.com
**subject:** Leland Brinker

Dear Vinky,

I had such a good time at the Mother's Day tea party you gave, and I know my mummy did, too. Anyway, I have a gigantic proposition for you. I'm working on the opening night party for this new club Candy, you've heard of it I'm sure, and I've GOT to have your client Leland there. It's sweet sixteen-themed, and we have a birthday girl there and everything. She's Patch Flood (the *real* Hottest Private-School Boy)'s little sis, Flan, and she's adorable, and she's a HUGE Leland fan. How great would it be if he showed up as her SURPRISE birthday date. Genius, right? Looking forward to your thoughts.

Liesel

**from:** vinky.morningside@vm.com
**to:** liesel@ddrpr.com
**subject:** RE: Leland Brinker

Okay, he's in, and I talked him into forgoing his usual appearance fee for the publicity opportunity, only because I've known you since you were a baby. I mean, you're still a baby! But since you were, like, literally a baby. We'll need wardrobe approval and a picture of this Flan person by tomorrow• and, of course, he'll only be able to fit in about an hour, MAYBE an hour and 15 min.
VM

**confession: sometimes when i hear the phrase "older guy," my ex-boyfriend pops into my head**

Life can change all of a sudden—one moment you're just another eighth grader waiting for high school to come around, and the next you're on the verge of being part of a whole scene. I could feel this happening to me, and I felt all excited and weird about it at the same time.

And it happened so randomly. I was just trying to find a party that I could take an old friend to, and it ended up being this Florence junior Liesel Reid's sweet sixteen and the next thing I know, I'm friends with a TV star and Liesel wants to be like best friends with me, too. She wants to throw *me* a sweet sixteen, even though I'm only fourteen. Not even fourteen, until Friday, when they are going to open a whole dance club with a party in honor of *my* birthday.

I didn't even meet Liesel at her party, she just

called me up a few hours after I got home from school on Wednesday and told me she thought my star was on the rise, and that she wanted to throw me this party that was going to be huge. And then she went on about all these celebrities who were going to be there, like Cressida Murphy and Wil Trayheart. Which might have sounded bizarre, except that now me and SBB from *Mike's Princesses* are sleepover friends, and all of that crazy party celebrity world doesn't seem so foreign anymore.

Liesel went on and on about how she worked for this public relations firm called DeeDee something or other, and so she had all these connections to turn my birthday into a huge event. And since her birthday party had been a huge event, I figured this was something she was probably right about. She said I should invite anybody I wanted and she'd put them on the list and that we could talk later about what I was going to wear. I asked if I could invite my whole eighth-grade class, and she said totally.

Pretty blow-your-mind fabulous, right? Like something a girl one of my brother's friends might love would do, right?

So why, forty-five minutes later, do I feel so panicky? Like, mind racing and palms sweating, so much so that when I put my hand up to my bedroom window, to sort of remind myself of the big, real world out there, it left this funny, sweaty streak. I looked at the pictures of Leland Brinker above my bed, and it seemed to me like the handiwork of a much younger person.

I decided to call Patch. He never seems to care one way or the other about being cool, so I thought he'd probably be a good person to calm me down.

"Hey Flannie," he said, after I'd said hello.

"Where are you?" I asked.

"At Jonathan's."

"Oh," I said. "What are you guys doing?"

"Just chilling."

"Well, could you go in the other room? There's something I want to ask you about in private."

"But they can't hear you," he said. "You're on the phone."

"Pa-*atch*," I whined, and he laughed and good-naturedly went in the other room. I explained the whole thing about Liesel to him, but he didn't seem very impressed.

"Just don't grow up too fast, okay?" he said when I'd finished.

"But Patch, you don't understand, what if

there's nobody there? I mean, what if nobody wants to come to my party?"

"Um, so what?"

"Patch!!"

"Okay, okay," he said. "I just don't see why you're freaking about this. I mean, Liesel said she's going to do a PR jobbie on your party, right? So lots of people will come. Probably way more people than you'd want to talk to in your whole life."

"But it's not about want to talk to! It's about quantity," I said, realizing how pathetic I sounded. "Will you just promise me that you'll come?"

"Sure."

"And will you make all of your friends come?"

Patch paused. "Which friends do you mean?"

"I don't know." I was blushing even though nobody was there to see me. "All of them?" I said, even though we both knew that Jonathan was the one I really cared about coming.

"Okay, I'll work on it. Arno just left to go to Liesel's house for dinner with the 'rents, so if Liesel is the one promoting this thing, it looks like he'll definitely be there whether you like it or not."

"Oh," I said. "Okay."

When I got off the phone, I lay back down on

the bed with the intention of telling myself I was hot enough to carry a whole opening night at a club in Chelsea, but before I could get very far my phone rang.

"Flannie, it's Livvie," Liv said. She was walking—I could hear all this chatter around her and the clicking of some sort of high heels. "I just got off the phone with SBB."

"Oh, really, what did she say?" For some reason, the way Liv was talking about SBB made me feel a little jealous or something. Which is silly, I know, but what can I say, it's true.

"Yeah, and she told me about this party of yours . . ."

"She did? Wow, Liesel works fast," I said, marveling that the news had already gotten to Liv. "But it's really exciting, don't you think?"

"Totally," Liv said. "I'm on my way home now with a big pile of magazines so we can start thinking about what to wear. But I was just so excited and I had to call, because I really think that this will be the time for certain connections between certain older guys and certain, ahem, younger girls to come out."

"Come . . . out?" Sometimes Liv doesn't talk all that logically, and I have to slow her down.

"Yeah, you know what I mean. For those

connections to be revealed, or become obvious, however you want to say it . . ."

"Wait, *what*?" I was so confused, but somehow I felt that Liv was telling me something very, very loaded. Not to mention how quickly we'd gone from talking about my party, which was supposed to be about me, to talking about something shady and Liv-related. "Liv, what are you talking about?"

"Well, Patch . . . and all his friends are going to be there, right?"

"Yeah, I mean hopefully . . ."

"So then it will be the perfect time to . . ."

A little electronic dying noise went whoosh and away, and then we were cut off. Liv had probably forgotten to charge her phone—she always hated doing menial things like that—and now for the first time I was really annoyed about it. I mean, how hard is it to plug that little thing in? Especially when you're going to drop bombs on one of your friends like that.

I mean, clearly when she said younger girl she was talking about herself. And who was this mystery older guy? And what did it have to do with Patch's friends?

As I curled back up in the pile of pillows on my bed, I realized something. I really was kind of jealous. Not of Liv being involved with my brother or one of his friends (apparently?), because that would be gross, but of all the attention Liv was getting. I mean, is that the only way to make guys notice you? Disappear for two years and come back with highlights?

True, that thing she'd said about older guys was totally vague and unclear, but I couldn't help but acknowledge that guys looked at her. All the time, wherever we went.

It was so unfair. *I* wanted to be with somebody. She's already had so many boyfriends, and I've really only had two. Remy was such a little jerk, I'm not even sure if that counts. And now she clearly thinks she's going to be one of the Insiders', or whatever they call themselves, girlfriends.

So freakin' unfair.

As you can see, I had already been on something of a roller coaster when my phone rang again. I picked it up without looking at the number, and then I heard a very familiar voice say, "Hey Flan."

"Oh, hi Jonathan," I said, so quietly, I should probably call it a whisper.

"How you been?"

"Okay, I guess," I said.

"I hear there's a party in the works for you," he said.

"Uh-huh," I said hopefully.

"Just be careful. You remember how much I got burned by that whole thing last spring . . ."

"Oh, yeah," I said. Was this what he had called me about?

"Anyway . . . I was wondering. Is Liv around?"

"No," I said, my voice rising sharply. Crap! Why am I such a spaz?

"Oh, okay," my ex-boyfriend, who used to be such a loyal friend and was now calling for Her Hotness herself, said. "Could you just maybe tell her I called looking for her?"

"Sure," I said, trying to keep my voice level.

I couldn't believe how lame this was. A small voice in my head told me not to get crazy and think that Jonathan's calling to talk to Liv had anything to do with that nonsense she had been talking on the phone—but then, some nauseating turn in my stomach told me that yes, these two events had everything to do with each other. Jonathan having a crush on Liv? I mean, how *lame* would that be?

And why did it suddenly seem like the most important thing in the world for him to come to my party?

**when parental approval is the last thing
a girl wants . . .**

"Arno . . . Wildenburger?" Jack Reid said, chewing over the name as he sipped from his glass of white wine. He was sitting in the sunken living room of his Fifth Avenue apartment. He was waiting with his wife, Meredith, and daughter, Liesel, for dinner to be served. They were all drinking white wine.

"Yeah, Daddy, you know! Of the Wildenbuwgers," Liesel said, gesticulating with her wineglass. "Yes, Daddy, *those* Wildenbuwgers."

Her mother patted her helmet of whitish blond hair and smiled as best she could. Her face was looking pretty stretched out these days. "That's wonderful, dear," she said. "Perhaps we can have a triple date!"

"Yeah, a little soon for that, Mom," Liesel said.

"Liesel, don't be silly," her father said, standing. His graying hair was slicked back and gray at the temples, and like all Reids, he was over six feet. He walked over to the platter of appetizers the maid had set up for them and artfully scraped some Morbier onto a cracker. "This is how the world works, my dear. This is how we do what we do."

"I'm not even sure we're dating yet!" Liesel said loudly, so that they would get her point.

"Oh, don't be modest, my dear," her mother said. She was wearing a white St. John knit suit with navy piping. "He's a good little acquisition."

"Mmmm . . . the Wildenburgers represent several newer artists we've been thinking about investing in," her father continued.

"Yes, even Hermann says our collection is beginning to look too uptown," said her mother, referring to their current art dealer. Hermann was seventy-six years old and always smelled like gin and toothpaste, even in the morning. "He allowed that we might want to consult some outside sources."

"Oh, I agwee with Hermann," Liesel said. "I'm sure DeeDee would, too."

"There you go," Liesel's mother said. "You can see what a good thing this is for us, that you're dating the Wildenburger boy."

Before Liesel could be exposed to more of this icky conversation, the doorbell rang. "I'll get it!" she yelled, so that the maid wouldn't even think about leaving the kitchen to let the guest in.

As she hurried to the foyer, she tried to banish the foreboding creepy feeling her parents were giving her by being so into her latest hookup. Because that was just gross.

"Awno!" she yelled, throwing the door open and pulling him to her by the shirt.

"Hey, Liesel," he said gloomily. He was wearing a threadbare button-down shirt with faint wildflowers on it, rolled to the elbows, and dark stained jeans with flip-flops. He brushed some hair out of his eyes, exposing his gorgeously angular features, bent his head, and attached his face to hers. She dragged him into the hall closet and they kept making out. Her hands went all over him, his hands went all over her.

When he pulled away, Arno said, "I don't know about this."

"Oh, please," Liesel laughed. She always laughed at things she didn't understand, and right now, she definitely had no idea why Arno was acting so un-Arno-like. "Awno," she said impatiently, "why do you think we're doing this?"

"Doing what?" Arno sounded genuinely confused.

"What we always do! Look, you can't even keep your hands off me!"

Arno pulled his hand out of Liesel's bra and sighed. "Don't you ever worry that our relationship doesn't have enough depth?"

"No," Liesel said, rearranging her DVF shirtdress. She wondered briefly if the brash, flirty Arno Wildenburger she had always known and heard about had been replaced by some morose, existential double. "I don't."

"I do," Arno said. "I'm trying to get more depth in my life, and I'm not sure that what we've got is up to that standard."

This time Liesel couldn't stop laughing. This was too rich. She held up a long, French-manicured finger and managed to get out "Hold on!" ' between guffaws.

"No, seriously," Arno said. "Like, I was just talking to my friend Patch about his ex-girlfriend Greta, who lives in California, and how crazy-intense their relationship is. They fight all the time about whether they should be together and how. It's really, you know, heavy, and he's just torn up about whether or not he can even be in a long-distance thing."

Liesel had gone from laughing to a simple smirk. "You guys sit around and talk about relationships all the time, don't you? If only all those girls out there obsessing over you knew—you're just like them!"

Arno straightened. "Am not."

"Okay, fine. *You're* not," Liesel said, turning from Arno indifferently and fussing with her hair.

"This is serious," Arno said. "If I don't stop my shallowness now, it could grow and grow and never stop. I mean, look how bad I looked after that whole Hottest Private-School Boy thing."

Liesel groaned. "Oh, dahling, you're not shallow. You just need better PR."

Arno looked unsure of his footing for a minute, and then he put his hand on Liesel's mini-butt and pulled her in for one last kiss.

"Come on," she said, pushing him away, but just enough to make her point. "Let me do this for you. Like rehab your image for you. All this worrying over being shallow really is not worth your time."

Arno shrugged. "I don't know . . ."

"Yes, you do," Liesel said, fixing him in her gaze. She knew that when their eyes met it had all the weight of fate, so she wasn't surprised at all when Arno gave her a little shrug of acquiescence.

"Okay," he said. "Let's see what you can do."

Liesel was laughing when she finally pulled him out of the closet and back toward her parents, who by now were probably sitting in the formal dining room and onto glasses of red wine. She didn't even care if she and Arno did have to go on a triple date with their parents, she was just glad she didn't have to hear Arno throwing around words like "shallow" and "deep" anymore.

"My parents are all excited to meet yours," Liesel said as they headed down the hall, hand in hand. "You know, they want to talk art deals."

"That's so shallow," Arno said.

"Okay, you know what?" Liesel said, clutching Arno's hand and wheeling him back to face her. "If I am going to represent you, then I insist that you not use that word anymore."

"But—"

Liesel leaned in, rested her forehead on Arno's, and gave him the look again.

"Okay," he said. "You're the boss. Now, can we just get this whole dinner thing over with?"

"Yes," Liesel said. "But one more thing? Those clothes. I'm going to have some samples sent to your place tomorrow, see if we can't get you back to that stylish stud I used to know . . ."

## a little pr multitasking from
## our very own liesel reid

**from:** liesel@ddrpr.com
**to:** vinky.morningside@vm.com
**subject:** RE: RE: Leland Brinker

Vink, you're amazing. We love Leland, and I just think it's perfect that he's going to be at the Candy sweet sixteen. But now that I've seen how much you can deliver for me, I'm going to need to call in a favor. You remember Arno Wildenburger, who *New York* magazine named Hottest Private-School Boy this year? He ended up looking sort of callow in that whole thing, and I'm going to be doing a little work on him image-wise. So I know you represent Eddie Turro of the Glories, and that they're playing shows at the Bowery Ballroom this week. Any chance we could get a nice little photo-op, with Arno and Eddie hanging backstage? It should look like they're talking about poetry or song lyrics. Tell me you're going to make it happen. Ciao, Lies

**from:** vinky.morningside@vm.com
**to:** liesel@ddrpr.com
**subject:** you got it

. . . but this time you owe me big-time, Liesel. Turns out Eddie's last album got panned by *New York*, so he's down to help Arno in any way he can. He wants Arno to come hang pre-show, and perform a song with him onstage. Do you love me OR WHAT? Be prepared to reciprocate, and make sure this Arno guy knows the words to Eddie's hit "Sally Seeking Solace." He absolutely has to be there by eight, and make sure he looks good, all right? I'll have the backstage pass delivered to DDR tomorrow. And tell DeeDee that she owes me lunch.
*sent wirelessly via Blackberry*

## a message to flan's eighth-grade class

from: liesel@ddrpr.com
to: undisclosed recipients
subject: Friday night at Candy

So by now you have all surely heard the buzz about this new hot club Candy, which is by and for people just like you—wild and crazy people who can't and don't care about getting into those tired old 21-and-over clubs!!! But you lucky people are on the list, because your friend Flan Flood is the big special sweet sixteen birthday girl of Candy's opening night, and she insisted you be on it. So take advantage of it, bunnies! And tell all your friends. They can come for a mere $30. Well worth it, in my opinion, considering the star power (Leland Brinker! Shhhhh!). So spread the word, and be there in your finest.

Your friend, the princess of buzz,

Liesel Reid

## even starlets have rocky love lives sometimes

SBB came home from a long day of shopping in which she had been photographed twice—that she knew of—and threw herself down on the Grobarts' worn black leather couch. "I'm finished!" she screamed, and waited for David's parents, Hilary and Sam, to come running into the living room from their respective offices.

It didn't take them long. Hilary came rushing in and put her arms around SBB and said, "What's wrong, dear heart?"

She was wearing a long belted cardigan and slacks, and she felt all sweatery and soft, just like SBB had always imagined a real mom would. "I couldn't stop myself," she said between sobs. "I had to go to Saks. And then as I was leaving I saw a paparazzi up on the mezzanine and he was shooting pictures of me."

"*No,*" Hilary said. "No wonder you're in such a state. That must have felt like a very real violation."

"It did." Sara-Beth hiccuped. She saw Sam Grobart appear in the doorway with a look of deep concern on his face. He took a step onto the old Persian rug and crossed his arms. She noticed that he was wearing one pair of glasses on his head and one on a chain around his neck. "But now Ric is going to fire me! Because I signed a piece of paper promising that I wouldn't be photographed going out until after the movie was shot and now they're going to tell me I can't do the movie and then my career will be over and . . . and . . . they *tricked* me!"

"That's absurd," Sam said. "You're going to be a big star. You're not disposable. There's only one of you in the whole world. I'm sure they will understand."

"That's right," Hilary said.

"But how do you know that?" SBB wailed.

"Because I know you," Hilary said, taking SBB's small face between her hands and giving her a serious look.

SBB sniffled, and then she batted her eyes and let a smile break out on her face. "You really think they're still going to let me be a star?"

"Of course they are," Sam said. "I'll put in a call myself, and explain that you were merely researching the role."

"That's true," SBB said, realizing that, in fact, she *had* been researching a role. Several times she had imagined stealing things from the racks at Saks, and her character in the new movie was a former Soviet assassin. SBB looked around the living room, which felt very green and peaceful because of all the house plants the Grobarts kept, and realized that going to Saks and thinking about shoplifting had been crucial to her developing understanding of the criminal mind.

"You have to start thinking of this as a positive change in your life," Hilary said, nodding along with herself. "Although we know that change is always painful."

"Yes, this is a serious role, and your ability to land a serious role should give you incredible confidence," Sam put in. "Though it also means giving up the comfort of your old role, your old . . . persona, if you will."

"And what this is really about is you, learning about yourself, what you're capable of . . . ," Hilary said, gesturing, her voice rolling as gentle as honey. SBB could feel her spirits rising along with Hilary's and Sam's tones.

"About you *shining*. Because, believe it or not, being a star and having a healthy psyche are not mutually exclusive."

"That's right. So all this anxiety about what it means to be in New York before you go on this trip of artistic realization, we just need to banish it. Tell it poof, be gone." Hilary's eyes glistened as she gave SBB a long, hopeful look. SBB had seen that look before, and she basically walked around craving it all the time. "Whatever needs to happen for you to be okay before Gdańsk, we'll make sure that happens."

SBB beamed up at the Grobarts, who were like her adoptive parents and personal gurus rolled into one person. Two people, whatever. She felt like the whole apartment, with its comfortable chairs and exotic wall hangings, was giving her a hug. "Thank you, guys," SBB said, wiping the last bit of moisture from her left eye.

That was when David walked through the door. He was holding a basketball under one arm, and his face was all exercised looking, and he had that adorable look of doofy confusion on his face that he always got when he came home to the happy surprise of the whole family together. His full lips hung open. SBB rushed over, wrapped her slender arms around his middle, and kissed him on the chest. "Guess what?"

"What?" David said.

"We're going to Europe early!"

"Wait—huh?" Hilary said.

SBB turned and smiled at Hilary. "I just think that's the best way to do away with the anxiety of being in New York—to leave New York this instant. Just drive to the airport right now and take off! Besides, they just *get* me in Europe." Sara-Beth turned to David and clapped excitedly. "Isn't this great?"

David looked like he had been hypnotized. He

stood there, in his sweat-stained T-shirt and basketball shorts, and said nothing for a long moment. Then the basketball fell to the floor. He didn't seem to notice it, and after another long silence, he said, very slowly, "I . . . don't . . . know . . . if . . . I . . . want to."

"*What?!*" Hilary and SBB said at once.

"Kiddo, what are you talking about?" Sam said.

"David, this is a tremendous opportunity," Hilary said. "For you, too. How many kids can put 'role in Ric Rodrickson flick' on their college apps?"

"Do you mean you don't want to go to Europe tonight?" SBB said, her voice rising to an anxious pitch. She really couldn't even deal with this right now. "Or do you mean you don't want to go . . . at all?"

"Everybody, everybody," Sam said, waving his hands, "we all need to calm down. I'm calling an emergency family therapy session. Now." They all went dutifully to the couches and sat down. "Does anyone need anything? Water? Coffee? No? Okay. David, you've clearly upset Sara-Beth. Would you like an opportunity to explain yourself?"

David closed his eyes and scratched the bare skin behind his ear. "I'm sorry," he said slowly, "I didn't mean to upset you."

"That's okay," SBB whispered. "It's just that I don't know why you wouldn't want to go to Gdańsk with me."

"It's not that I don't want to go to Gdańsk with *you*.

I just . . ." David looked up at his parents helplessly, like he was searching for an answer. They gave him hard stares. "Look, I just want to be a normal guy. I'm not sure running off to Gdańsk is me, you know what I mean?"

SBB threw her face into her hands and whimpered. Hilary rubbed Sara-Beth's back and removed the pencil that had been holding up her pile of dark curls. She pointed it at David and said, "No, mister, I don't think I do know what you mean."

"Um." David shook his head, like he was trying to shake off a bad prophecy. "Okay, here's an example. There's this party on Friday night that I wouldn't be able to go to if I went to Gdańsk. I mean, if I went early, like you're saying."

"What party could possibly be more important than my first serious job as a real actress?" SBB gasped, turning toward Sam and Hilary for support. "Do you not believe in me?"

"She has a point," Sam said.

"Well, I mean it's just an example. And of course I believe in you! But I think Flan is expecting you to go to this party, too. Her sweet sixteen? Remember, this Friday?"

"Oh . . . right," SBB said, her features coming together unpleasantly. She looked like another tantrum was hovering, but after a moment she threw up her hands and said, "Okay, I guess it's not the best idea to fly to Europe tonight."

Sam made a show of sniffing the air. "Is that sweet compromise I smell?" he said.

"Dad," David said sharply. He couldn't even bring himself to look at his father after that joke.

"Yeah," said SBB, "it's fine. We can go on Saturday, just like before. I'm sorry, David, that I made such a big scene about my little anxieties."

"Awww . . . ," Hilary said. She clasped her hands together and pressed them against her cheek. "So, we're all okay, then? And David, I want to say that we totally support your desire for . . . normalness."

"That's right," Sam said.

"Oh, me too!" Sara-Beth said. "David, not only do I support your normal side, I love you for it. Now come on, I want to see if this suit I bought you for Gdańsk fits." Sara-Beth slapped her forehead. "Silly me! I mean, if this suit I bought you for Flan's party fits."

**sbb is only good with her own secrets**

*"Hey, it's Flan, I miss you already, so leave me a message!"*
"Flan! It's Sara-Beth. Guess what. Liesel just called me and she said that she got Leland Brinker for Friday night. Leland's coming to your party! Are you psyched or what? Kiss!"

*"Hey, it's Flan, I miss you already, so leave me a message!"*
"Flan, it's Liesel. I hear Sara-Beth spilled the beans on a very special indie star who will be attending your party, but oh well. It's still exciting. Listen, would you call me when you can? We've got some details to iron out, cutie-pie. Ciao, ciao."

Liv had taken to always wearing sunglasses, even indoors, just like her new pal Sara-Beth Benny. She was wearing them now as she strode through the aisles of Bloomingdale's, and it was actually really helping her do what she was trying to do. Which was pretend to look at clothes in the BCBG section for potential Friday night outfits, while in fact keeping an eye on Flan.

Because Flan was not only her best friend from elementary school, but also the little sister of Liv's secret lover, Patch. If Flan found out that Liv had kissed Patch's friend David, then her whole golden couple dream would be out the window like that.

So Liv watched as Flan had yet another phone conversation with Liesel about the big birthday bash, and tried to listen in. She was listening to hear any hint that maybe Flan knew more than she was letting on about the whole kissing David accident, or whether she knew any little thing about Patch's plan to take things slow.

After all, was it really possible that Patch had confessed nothing of these momentous events to his little sister, that he had asked her for no advice? She seemed so clueless about the whole Liv and Patch thing in general that it was hard to know what was an act and what wasn't.

Flan flipped her phone shut and came bounding back over toward Liv. "One word," she said, pulling her hair up to ponytail height and opening her blue eyes wide. "Elephants."

Liv scrunched her nose. "Elephants? Isn't that sort of . . . inhumane?"

Flan rolled her eyes and let her hair fall down. "Noooo. It's a baby elephant. The most spoiled baby elephant in all the world, probably. And Liesel said DeeDee Rakoff is paying an arm and a leg, so I'm sure it's well taken care of."

"DeeDee Rakoff is paying for it?"

"Well the firm, whatever . . ." Flan shrugged. "Anyway, did you find anything?"

"Not really," Liv said, pushing her sunglasses up her nose and taking a long strand of artificially suntouched hair and twirling it. "But I'm sure the dress for you is here. Somewhere."

"It's gotta be," Flan said, exhaling and then wondering how to bring up her Jonathan suspicions. They both started moving down the aisle, pushing hangers back rapid-fire. After a few minutes without finding anything, Flan looked up, fixed Liv in her stare, and said, "So, I talked to Jonathan yesterday night . . ."

"Oh, goodie," Liv said without thinking. She paused to look at a turquoise dress with a belted waist. Then she thought of something. "Wait, he called to talk to you, right?"

Liv looked up, and she and Flan appraised each other awkwardly. Flan took a breath and then said, "No, actually. He was looking for you. I was supposed to tell you last night, but I guess I forgot somehow. Maybe 'cuz it seemed so . . . strange."

"Well, what did he say he wanted?" Liv's mind was racing with all the things Jonathan and she might have discussed, who they might have told, and what the consequences of all these combinations were.

"He didn't," Flan said sharply. They advanced down the row of dresses.

"Huh, that's funny . . ." Liv studied Flan's face, which didn't look like it could conceal anything, and then decided that Jonathan really hadn't told her anything unusual. She nodded in agreement with herself. "You know what I bet? I bet he wanted to talk to you, and then when he heard your voice he got all bashful-like and then he made up something about wanting to talk to me."

"You think?" Flan looked dubious, but she didn't look suspicious anymore, which was good.

"Definitely. I've never talked to Jonathan in my life. What else could it be?"

"Maybe . . . ," Flan said, narrowing her eyes like she was trying to see a kernel of truth out on the horizon. Liv didn't seem to be involved with Jonathan, but then she certainly seemed to be trying to throw Flan off *some* trail. That whole bashful thing was total and utter BS.

Liv twisted her hair and moved forward. "So . . . Jonathan didn't say anything about David?"

*"David?!"* Flan almost jumped, so surprised was she to hear his name in this conversation. He was the only one of her brother's friends who had a real girlfriend, not to mention a girlfriend who was in a whole different league. She wondered if David could possibly be the older guy in question, and then decided there was just no way. "No . . . Why in the world would he mention David?"

Flan watched Liv smile broadly, and knew immediately that she was concealing something. And it pretty much had to have something to do with Jonathan.

"Oh, I don't know. Maybe he was calling about SBB, and because of the whole David thing, and well, you know . . ." Liv shrugged and felt free and happy, because now she knew for sure that Flan, and thus Patch, knew nothing about that treacherous kiss.

"Know what? That doesn't make any sense," Flan said. "If he was calling to find out something about

SBB, then why didn't he just ask to talk to her? Are you . . . *lying* to me?"

"What? I couldn't hear you. . . . Oh, hold on. Maybe this would look nice on you!" Liv tossed a brown halter dress with seashells sewn all over it across the aisle at Flan. She smiled brightly and innocently, and hoped that Flan would be distracted by her pick. Then she went back to combing the dresses on the racks, and waited for the whole unpleasant conversation to be over. She had gotten what she needed out of it, after all, and she didn't know what Flan was making a fuss about.

Liv was distracted from this series of thoughts by an incoming text message from her mom that read *where are you young lady!?* so she didn't even notice Flan running toward the dressing room and slamming the door behind her.

## i break down in bloomingdale's

Maybe it was the party pressure, maybe it was the thought of Leland Brinker blowing out candles on my birthday cake, maybe it was that I'd skipped lunch . . . who knows. But as soon as I hit the dressing room at Bloomie's, I was a falling down mess.

And then I looked at this ugly brown seashell thing that Liv had given me, and I realized that I was having trouble trusting my best friend from elementary school. And that's just never a good moment in an almost-fourteen-year-old-girl-on-the-verge-of-having-her-sweet-sixteen-party's life. Know what I mean?

So I sat there, crying, tears running down my face, making it all pielike and ugly, and I looked at this dress and I thought: (A) That dress is ugly; (B) Liv picked it for me, so she must want me to look ugly; thus (C) Liv must be having a secret something with Jonathan.

Because suddenly I didn't want to meet Leland Brinker. All I wanted was Jonathan. Is that strange?

I mean, you would do the same thing I did, right? Which was that I curled up on the floor of the dressing room and I called my brother. It took him too many rings to answer, and when he picked up, he said, "Hey Flannie."

"Hiiiii . . ." I knew I sounded like a baby, but I couldn't help it. Patch always had the magic ability to calm me down, just by being him, and I was waiting for the magic to hit. "Patch, are you coming to my party tomorrow?"

"Yeah," he said in that baked-on-the-beach voice of his, "of course I am. Why? You thinking of bailing?"

"No—how can I?" I tucked my legs up against my chest and tried not to look at my reflection in the, like, twenty-five dressing room mirrors that were facing me down ominously. "Patch, I don't know if I'm ready for this."

"You mean a big party at a New York City club, with celebrities, and energy drinks, in your honor? Nah, you'll love it."

"I don't think so," I said in a small voice.

Patch sighed. "Listen, Flannie Bug, I'm out skating with Mickey and his new girlfriend and his old girlfriend."

"You mean Philippa?" For a moment, I put my self-pity on hold, because that was too weird. Philippa had been Mickey's girlfriend for as long as I can remember, and her identity has always kind of been defined by the outsized personality of her boyfriend. Then she turned lesbian or something, which was so obviously just her trying to get a life. "That's weird."

"Yeah, she's really good, too. Or at least, she's trying to be good. I think she hates Mickey's new girlfriend, and doesn't want to be shown up by her."

"Oh," I said.

"So . . . are you okay? Sounds like you're being kind of a baby."

I decided to ignore that little bit of brotherly judgment. "Whatever, I'm fine," I said. The Patch magic was starting to work.

"Oh yeah?"

"Yeah," I said, straightening up and forcing myself to think if anything could be done about my pudgy crying face. "There's just one thing I want you to do for me."

"Name it."

"Make sure Jonathan is at my party, okay?"

There was a pause on the other line, and then Patch said, "Okay, you got it."

"Is he still going out with little miss freckle face, by the way?"

"Why do you ask?"

"Oh, no reason, just curious."

"Yeah, well, I think he broke it off. That raw-food-soup-at-nine-a.m. thing was a deal breaker."

"And has he said anything about any other girls?"

"Um . . . I guess he muttered something about having a crush on somebody, but . . ."

I gave myself a look in the closest dressing room mirror, which was pleasantly flattering, and decided that it really didn't matter whether there was something maybe going to happen between Jonathan and Liv, or if he was mumbling about having a crush on her. It hadn't mattered that the tree-hugger girl liked him, either—she happened, and now she was gone. I looked in that mirror and I decided that I was going to stop acting like a little girl and get myself together for this party. I was going to be glamorous and exciting, and I was going to get Jonathan back.

I told myself, Look at yourself! You are so the kind of girl one of the Insiders would love. I was just going to have to start putting it out there.

"Are you there?" Patch said.

"Yeah, sorry. So you'll definitely make sure that Jonathan comes to the party?"

"Sure."

"Great," I said. "You're the best! Okay, back to dress shopping!"

When I emerged from the dressing room, I saw Liv standing there with a big pile of dresses in her arms and a face full of regret.

"I sorry," she said, just like we always used to when we were nine. And just like that, I knew that it was all going to work out for me. Pretty soon, she was going to see that I was just as glamorous as she, or SBB, or Liesel were, and then she would regret that she ever had a secret crush on Jonathan that she tried to keep from me. "How did the dress look?" she asked.

"Oh . . . I didn't even try it on. I don't know if I can try anything else on for right now."

"I hear you," Liv said brightly. "What do you say we go downtown and get some hijiki burgers at Dojo?"

"Okay," I said, because I had to admit that part of my freak-out was due to the hunger currently

136

gnawing its way through my stomach. Then Liv grabbed my hand and we walked toward the exit.

For a very brief moment, Liv's niceness made me wonder if maybe I was crazy, and I thought about confessing the whole thing to her, about how I'd—briefly, insanely—thought that she and Jonathan were involved, and how that made me realize that I wanted him back. But then Liv started swinging her big, plain brown Bloomie's bag, and said, all fake nonchalant-like, "So, what were you and Patch talking about?"

There was this buzzing in my ear. I smacked it, but it wouldn't go away. It was like a little voice in my head telling me that telling Liv every last thing wasn't the best idea anymore.

I shrugged. "Nothing," I said. "I'm starved. Let's just take a cab downtown, okay?"

## liesel reid, pr superstar

Manhattan was full of honking cars and steaming hot dog stands, but you wouldn't have known that up by the rooftop pool of a certain building, on Park in the mid-70s, where everything was blue skies and quiet, except for the clinking of ice cubes in afternoon cocktails.

Liesel flipped over onto her belly and unsnapped her bikini top, even though her skin was basically tan resistant. She just liked the whiff of danger she got from having her bathing suit top undone in public.

This was just another part of a thoroughly busy and exhilarating day out promoting Candy, the new Chelsea club for underage socialites that she was working on as the most trusted and adored intern in the history of DDR PR. She took a piece of papaya from the small table set up next to her poolside recliner and sucked on it thoughtfully. It was a blissfully clear day, and up on top of her old friend Mimi Rathbone's building, there was just a touch of a breeze.

"So, are you coming or what?" Liesel said eventually.

Mimi twisted her long horsetail of whitish blond hair into a knot on the back of her head. "Lies, you know I'd do anything for you. But an underage club? Filled with guys our own age? It just sounds kind of lame to me."

Liesel removed the papaya from her mouth and took a sip of her Perrier. "I get it. I understand that. But aren't you tired of older guys sometimes? Don't you sometimes just want to dance and look fabulous in a room full of fabulous people?"

"I guess," Mimi said doubtfully. She was lying on her back and wearing a turquoise bikini and Prada shades, and she looked ridiculously exercised for a seventeen-year-old. Liesel recognized Mimi as a new money kind of Upper East Side blonde, while Liesel herself was a classic Upper East Side blonde. But Mimi had a following, and Liesel needed her and all her little minions at the Candy opening.

"Listen, I guarantee this party is going to be covered in all the gossip columns. Know why?" She leaned over in her chair, toward Mimi, and whispered, "I got Leland Brinker."

"Noooo . . . ," Mimi gasped, turning toward Liesel and pushing her glasses on top of her head. "For a dirty downtown folk singer, he is so delicious. I would totally hook up with him."

"I know!"

"Okay, I'm in." Mimi took a sip of her Perrier and got a far-off look in her eyes. "So, how many people do I get to put on the guest list?"

"Sugar, you just tell me who you want."

Both girls paused to take in the late afternoon, chlorine-tinged laziness of it all. A pool boy stopped by to replenish their bubbly water, and when he was gone Mimi said, "I heard a rumor."

"I love rumows," Liesel said.

"Me too. Except this one gives me the creeps."

"Oh, really?" Liesel said, adjusting her bikini bottom ever so slightly.

"Yeah, this one's about Arno." Mimi dropped her sunglasses to the bottom of her ski jump nose. "Arno Wildenburger. And you."

Liesel had been thinking about the rebirth of Arno Wildenburger, hot private-school boy, all day, and she didn't like the way Mimi was saying his name. But if Liesel had learned one thing during her time at DeeDee Rakoff, it was how to set the tone of any conversation to her advantage. "My, that one got around quick," she said casually. "But it makes sense because people just love to talk about Awno."

"Yeah, especially when our whole social circle saw

him leaving the Boat House bathroom with you. With all the people there, I'm surprised it didn't show up on the front page of the *Post*," Mimi said, with maybe a tad more nasty than was necessary.

"I guess I'll have to work harder next time," Liesel said without missing a beat. "*Entre nous*, he's totally on the verge of being hot again. And I'll keep hooking up with him in restaurant bathrooms until he is!"

Mimi made a snorting noise. "Okay, fine, but just remember what happened with that whole Hottest Private-School Boy thing. I thought he was totally hot, too, until it turned out he wasn't."

"Oh, that whole Hottest Private-School Boy thing is such a joke. DeeDee always says so," Liesel said, ending the conversation so that she could return to tanning in peace.

After all, tonight was the night when Arno was going to party backstage with Eddie Turro of the Glories and then make a surprise appearance onstage with him. His rep was going to be totally back in order after that, and Mimi Rathbone was just going to have to stew in all her jealous, fake-blond juices.

## checking in on the old new hot guy

*"Wildenburger, talk to me."* BEEP

"Awno, it's Lies. I know you're probably about to head over to the Bowery, to hang with Eddie and the boys, but I wanted to make sure that package from Rogan got to you with the special outfit. Oh my God, you're going to look hot hot hot. Call me if you want me to come over and tie your tie, okay? Ciao, ciao."

## philippa isn't kidding around anymore

"So, that was fun," Sonya said, coming out from the kitchen with a six-pack of Tecate under her arm. Her black hair was piled up on top of her head and speared with a stick, and she was wearing jean cutoffs that were way too big for her and rolled up at the hem, and a threadbare camisole. Philippa took a look at her and decided that Sonya definitely didn't think what had just happened was fun. There was definitely some sarcasm lurking under that word.

"Way," Mickey said, grabbing one of the cans and drinking from it. "I didn't even know you could skate till this afternoon." They were sitting on the roof of the Pardos' Perry Street compound, which was decorated with palm trees and various wood sculpture/chair hybrids. The sun was going down in a hazy blaze of glory. Mickey was wearing a Misfits T-shirt and absently rubbing his round belly. "Isn't that weird?" Mickey said, as though he were still sort of stunned by it himself. "That

I went out with her for so long and I never knew that she could skateboard?"

Sonya sat down in one of the chairs and put her feet on the varnished tree stump table at the center of their chair circle. "That is odd," she said, and swiveled her head to give Philippa a piercing look. Things had not gone smoothly with them during the skateboarding exhibition.

"Well, I didn't know Mickey skated, either," Philippa said quickly. "Turns out he does sometimes, with his friend Patch. Same with me, except with other friends."

"Are you sure you haven't been practicing all week?" Sonya said, dropping a devilish wink.

"Oh, yeah, like I would even have the time," Philippa said indignantly, realizing immediately that it didn't sound like a resounding rebuttal. In truth, she had only spent the better part of a morning learning a few tricks with some skater dykes she'd met through Stella, and it had been worth it. While Sonya had been fearless and fun out there, she hadn't really known how to do anything. And Philippa knew that her few well-executed tricks had made Mickey stop feeling sorry for her and start paying attention to her. In the old way.

"Anyway, it's not like anyone's born knowing how to skateboard. Don't you think Mickey would have had some idea that you could ollie?" Sonya said, swigging from her Tecate. "I mean, how long did you go out?"

"Two years," Mickey and Philippa said at once.

"But we basically have been flirting since my family moved to that house"—Philippa pointed to a rooftop directly across from them, and smiled unconsciously—"when I was nine."

"Wow," Sonya said, "that is a long time." She studied her beer for a moment and then said, "So how is it you just suddenly became a lesbian, Philippa?"

"Um, I guess it was something that I've been wondering about for a long time . . . ," Philippa said defensively.

"Oh, just wondering about? I bet Stella didn't think you were just wondering," Sonya said with a smirk.

"I didn't say that," Philippa snapped back, cocking her head. With a few words, Sonya had declared that the simmering tensions of the day had now brought them to full-fledged warfare. And Philippa wasn't about to stand down on her own turf. "I really went out with Stella. It was for real, until she turned all crazy and also kind of boring on me."

"Whoa, whoa," Mickey said, standing up and crushing his beer can underfoot. He took another and swigged before he said, "Nobody wants to hear about this, girls."

"I do," Sonya said. "See, this may all be a little joke for you, but I've had a really hard time being bisexual, because nobody believes being a bisexual is a real thing. Well, you know why? Because of people like you, who are basically straight and then just go around toying with lesbian identity for brief periods of time and then try and get back with their old boyfriends."

"Yo, I need to whiz," Mickey said before turning and jogging toward the edge of the roof. "Into the Fradys' yard!" he called behind him.

But Philippa wasn't going to bite at that one—she had a much scarier fish to worry about. She and Sonya were still sitting on the sculptural chairs, but they were ready to pounce on each other at any second.

"I really am a lesbian, so you can just take all this self-righteousness and shove it!"

"Oh, come on, be honest for once," Sonya said. "You've been competing with me all day. It was you who set me up with Mickey, and now you regret it. Right? Am I right?"

Philippa had her skirt bunched up in her palms, and she felt closer to swatting another girl than she had pretty much ever. "So what if I do?" she said with a toss of her head.

"You are such a fake lesbian!" Sonya screeched. Mickey remained focused on pissing off the roof, which Philippa knew was just a ruse to stay far, far away from a conflict that was ready to boil over.

"I am not!" Philippa screamed. "I just happen to be a little more open-minded than you are! I just happen to fall in love with people, not genders!"

Before Philippa knew what hit her, she was wrestling with Sonya on the ground. Sonya had a fistful of her hair, which really hurt, not to mention the rockiness of the ground, which was covered with pebbles. Philippa had had a few skating lessons, but no lessons in how to fight girl-on-girl, and it was all she could to do to get a few innocuous slaps in before Mickey came hustling over from the other side of the roof and pulled Sonya off her.

Philippa looked up from the ground and saw that Sonya was heaving and red-faced. It looked like she was really pissed. Also, she had little pebbles embedded in her skin, and Mickey was brushing them off, sort of gently, it seemed. It dawned on Philippa for the first time that Mickey might actually be angry, and at her.

Eventually Mickey extended a hand and pulled Philippa up to her feet. There was a look on his face that Philippa had never seen before. Weirdly, since she was the one who had just been attacked and thrown to the ground, Philippa found herself saying, "Are you okay, Mickey?"

He shook his head slowly. "Not really. This shit's just totally out of hand. I mean, you're straight, you're gay, you hook me up with a great girl, you're straight again." He sighed. "You are straight messing with my head."

Sonya put an arm around Mickey and gave him a comforting back rub.

Philippa had not only never felt this unwelcome in the Pardo home, she had never been in the position of apologizing to Mickey—usually it was the exact opposite. "Can't you understand that I just happen to be a lesbian who's in love with Mickey Pardo?" she whispered.

"Um, not really," Mickey said. He shook his head, and they all seemed to realize that it had grown dark at the same time. "I need some time, for real, so I think you better leave."

Philippa took one sad look at Mickey, standing there being half embraced by Sonya, and then she did the only thing she could do. She tried to put her chin in the air a little bit and leave the Pardos' with some scrap of dignity.

## i have nightmares sometimes

The night before my birthday, I could hardly sleep. Liv lay next to me snoring away. Maybe that had something to do with it. Or maybe it had more to do with the fact that my dreams went something like: Jonathan and Liv fly in a private plane to some Caribbean island or other, and I get discovered hiding under a seat and the pilot comes back and opens a hatch and tosses me into the ocean while Jonathan and Liv have a champagne toast. I tossed, I turned, and finally I pulled myself out of bed and stumbled down the old maid's stairs toward the kitchen with the hope of finding some benevolent fairy or other waiting there with a glass of warm milk.

Instead, I found my sister, February, nodding off in a chair with a half-smoked cigarette dangling from her mouth. Her short black hair was choppy and jutted in several directions, and her mascara was definitely running a little bit. She was wearing a silver sequined sheath dress and ripped black tights. Maybe it was that I was half asleep, but the whole thing looked surreal. I went over, took the cigarette out of her mouth, and tossed it into the sink. She opened her eyes slowly.

"Flannie . . . I must have fallen asleep," she said, smiling at me. She took her feet off the table, and when she did, her collection of silver anklets made a loud jangling noise.

"Where have you been?" I asked.

"Working," she said. By work, Feb means promoting. She's out every night, promoting various clubs, which basically means socializing and telling your friends how to think, but they pay her real money to do it. And then during the day she designs her own line of jewelry, so she's very busy. "I hear there's a big party for you tomorrow," she said.

"Yeah," I said. Feb can be pretty opinionated about what's cool and what's not, and I really didn't want to talk about it right then.

But she just stood up, put me in the chair, and said, "That's nice."

"I guess."

"Why are you up right now, anyway?" she said.

"Couldn't sleep." I shrugged.

"You want me to heat you up some milk?" she said, patting my head. I nodded, and she went to the fridge and took out a bottle of milk and poured it into a saucepan. As she heated it up, she lit another cigarette and smoked contemplatively. "I don't think I can come. To the party," she said. "Work."

"Oh . . . that's okay," I said, suddenly disappointed. I hadn't really thought that she would come anyway, but now that I'd heard it out loud, it made me sad.

"But I'm glad I caught you," she said as she poured the milk from the saucepan into a mug and handed it to me. I took a sip and felt my mind unclench and my body begin to relax. I hadn't had warm milk in a long time. "Do you know what time it is?" Feb asked after I had taken a few sips.

I shook my head, and then we both looked at the microwave clock as it flipped to midnight. Feb gave me a big red-lipstick smile and came over and kissed me on the head. "Happy birthday, little sister," she said.

When I finished my milk, I went back upstairs and fell right into a deep sleep, and it was as though the whole scene in the kitchen with Feb and her ripped stockings was a dream.

## liesel gets an unpleasant phone call

Liesel came home early on Thursday night, feeling she had sufficiently spread the word about Candy, her new friend Flan, and her old new boyfriend, Arno. She had a light dinner of salmon tartare with the cook in the kitchen, drank two liters of spring water, and climbed into bed to watch twenty minutes of *The Philadelphia Story*. She always liked to absorb a little Hepburn before any really big event.

She had put her eye mask on and was happily floating into some much-needed beauty sleep, when one of her cell phones started vibrating. She pushed her eye mask back onto her head, looked over at her nightstand, realized it was her work phone, and checked the caller ID. "Vinky!" she cried, answering it. "What's happening? It's kind of late."

"Reid, you've screwed me!" Vinky screeched. "And you of all people should know that there's no sleep in PR."

"Vinky," Liesel said, her heart racing, "what's the matter?"

"What do you mean, *what's the matter!?*" Vinky snapped. Liesel had known Vinky for years, because they had the same godmother, and Liesel could just picture her marching down the street in a white trench and spiked Manolos and a flowing mane of blond hair. At twenty-eight, Vinky was Liesel's model of how to rise quickly into a public relations legend. "Your little friend Arno never showed up tonight, and he made Eddie look like an idiot. *That's* what happened."

"But how . . . ?" Liesel sat up. She was trying not to say too much before she fully understood the situation.

"Well, Eddie called him onto the stage, just like we talked about, and Arno didn't come out, because he never turned up, so poor Eddie was just left there by himself with nothing to say. And you know Eddie isn't that bright, so of course the whole thing was painful. Painfully, *painfully* awkward."

"Oh deah, how could he . . . ?"

"I don't know, darling, but whatever you owed me before, quadruple it!"

"Vinky, I'm so—" Liesel's head was full of questions about Arno, and why he had ditched the Eddie thing, but she wasn't so muddle-headed that she wasn't going to try and smooth this one out. Unfortunately, Vinky wouldn't let her get a word in.

"Oh, *can* it, Reid. And don't think I didn't consider pulling Leland from your little club opening tomorrow. I did try, in fact, but it seems that our friend Leland has developed a crush on Flan because of that stupid picture you sent."

"Well," Liesel said, struggling to stay diplomatic, "thank you for that, Vinky."

"You're welcome. Now I've got to go take poor Eddie over to Schiller's for a nice late dinner and some sympathy. Calm him down, reconvince him that he's the next Bono."

"Please tell him I'm sorry about this whole debacle."

"I will," Vinky said hotly. "And say hello to your mother for me."

After Liesel got off the phone, she sunk back into her mountain of silk-covered goose down. What a nightmare. She didn't know whether she was more angry at Arno for embarrassing her in front of Vinky, or for missing the opportunity to make a big, public show of how hot he still was.

She gave it a few minutes, just to calm herself down. Liesel firmly believed that anger released an ugly chemical into the bloodstream that would leave her with stringy hair and dull skin, and she really had to look great for the event tomorrow no matter what.

When she was relatively not filled with rage anymore,

she reached for her personal phone, clicked through her phone book to *Stud*, and hit CALL.

"Yo," Arno said when he answered.

"Yo?!" she snapped back.

"Oh. Hey, you. How's your night?"

"Well, blissful, until the phone call I got from Vinky Morningside a few minutes ago. She's fuwious, as well she should be, that you didn't show up for your cameo at the Bowery tonight."

"Huh?" Arno said. She could hear video game noises in the background.

"Where are you?"

"Patch's."

"Oh," Liesel said. "I get it. I set you up with a big night hanging with Eddie Turro and the Glories, and you thought it would be more fun to stay home and play video games with the friends you've had forever?"

"Oh, that . . . ," Arno said distractedly. "Yeah, I guess I just thought the Glories were a little too pop for me to mesh with them."

"Oh, really!?"

"Yeah . . . ," Arno said. Liesel could hear congratulations going around for some big video game moment in the background. "Anyway, your big event is tomorrow night right? Am I your date?"

"Yes, you are!" Liesel yelled. "And believe me," she said bitterly, "it's going to be a fun freaking time!"

Then she hung up the phone and threw it into the covers piled up at the end of her bed, where it disappeared.

**my big day. whoo-freaking-hoo.**

By this time in the school year even the vale-dictorian has forgotten how to do homework, and so I guess it was natural enough that all any-body could talk about was summer and parties and, well, one very big nightclub opening. I mean, I guess some speech in front of your junior high teachers and classmates just can't compete with that. All anyone wanted to talk about, this particular Friday afternoon in June, was whether so-and-so was actually going to be at my party and what I was going to wear and how crazy it was that I had gotten them on the list. By the time I had collected my books and headed for home, I almost felt like this stupid party had hap-pened already.

Nobody seemed to remember that the whole reason for the party was my birthday—nobody had even sung me a song or wished me a happy one yet. Not to mention, I didn't even have a dress. When I woke up this morning, I just decided that I'd wear my same old yellow sundress and give the anxiety a rest.

But that was before I got home from school and saw the package.

SBB was sitting on my front steps, and the package was in her lap. Two, actually: a white box with a big white bow around it, and a smaller, pink box on top. SBB was wearing a black djellabah that could have been a shirt but was, on her, a dress, with her black wig and her black sunglasses. She was like the mod version of my favorite TV character.

"Hey, beautiful!" she said when she saw me.

"Hi, SBB," I said, quietly because I know she gets freaked out whenever her name gets uttered in public.

"Have you been treating yourself decadently?" she asked with a bent head that suggested I was in trouble if I hadn't been.

"Yeah." I shrugged. "Whatever, it's just my birthday. I'm going to have a lot of them."

"That's some crazy talk! This is the birthday all your other birthdays from here on out are going to have to compete with. Here, take this," she said, handing me the pink box. "Go ahead, peek!"

"Oh my God, these are so delicious looking!" I almost wanted to cry, because when I looked at the cupcakes in the box I realized that SBB actually knew that it was my birthday and what birthdays were about. I mean, warm milk from my sister is pretty rare, but still. Sometimes a girl wants a cupcake. I was so touched that I stupidly added: "But wait, aren't you not allowed to eat sweets until after shooting?"

"Oh, it's a birthday. On *birthdays* I'm allowed."

I smiled at SBB—I kind of couldn't believe she was here, for the pre-party stuff, but I was glad she was. "And the other box?" I asked.

"For that, we have to go inside," she said sternly. Then, lowering her voice to a whisper: "But between you and me, Liesel told me I had to be here at four to sign for the messenger, and I saw where the package was coming from."

"Oooo! Where? Where?"

"One little word for you, beautiful. Marc."

I swear to God, we both jumped up and down like children. I know, I know! I wouldn't have believed that a TV star/burgeoning starlet would jump up and down about clothes she could have had for free, anytime, but I was there, and I promise, it really happened.

"Come on, you," she said. "Let's go make you look like a star."

The house was oddly empty of people, but Patch had promised me so many times that he would be at the party, and that he would bring Jonathan, that I just had to stop worrying about that already. When we got up to my room, Sara-Beth and I shared a cupcake—she said there would be cake later, and we should save room by only having half a cupcake now—and then she poured us champagne from the bucket of chilled Veuve Clicquot that had somehow appeared in my bedroom.

"Cheers to you," she said.

"Thank you," I said, and then we clinked glasses and opened the box.

The dress shone up at me from its place in the box like a solar eclipse—I swearsies, it was like a religious moment or something. It was a cocktail dress made out of champagne-colored silk and tulle, and it had this empire waist, and this crazy big skirt, and this large, decadent bow right under the bodice.

"Okay, sit down," SBB said. She pushed me into the chair in front of my vanity, which had been turned into a movie-set-like makeup HQ, and went to work.

I tried to look seriously into the mirror as the most glamorous person I know did my makeup. After a few moments of quiet toner cleansing and cover-up applying, SBB said, "So, have you thought of things to talk about with Leland?"

"Oh, Leland . . ." Wait, was I supposed to have been taking that really and truly seriously? I mumbled something I hoped would make sense, along the lines of, "Well, I don't know if I can . . . be his secret date anymore. Or if he can be mine or whatever."

"You don't know if you can what?" SBB said. She was wielding a large blush brush, and for a second I was afraid to tell her that my romantic goals had been downgraded. She would think that my wanting Jonathan would be less glamorous, less irreverent, less like the kind of girl that guys love, right?

"If I can, you know, go for Leland anymore," I said at last.

"Close your eyes," SBB said. I could feel her start to apply eyeliner. "That's good, he's really sort of a dick. I didn't want to tell you before, because this is *your* night, but after Leland and I hooked up he never called me again. His songs are all sincere and emotional, but he's not like that in real life. And you know I totally am the peppermint girl on the brink, right? Yeah, that's a real funny joke."

"I'm sorry," I said. I felt like a total jerk for ever having been into him at all. Even if it was from a pretty big distance. "I only liked that album the first time I listened to it anyway."

SBB raised my chin with her hand and looked into my eyes. She didn't look like it bothered her at all. "That's okay, beautiful. He's a glorified reality star who nobody will remember in two years. But my question is, who's going to be your birthday date now?"

"Well . . ." I bit my lip and watched SBB closely for approval. "I think I might still be into my ex. Jonathan."

"You mean David's friend! Oh my God, that's so great. When David and I get back from Gdańsk, we totally have to double-date and you can hear all our stories. That would be so much fun, just the four of us!"

"I know!" I said, suddenly imagining a whole string of glamorous evenings. With the guy I'd always known and trusted and been able to be my goofiest self around. I guess maybe that wasn't glamorous . . . but it seemed nice anyway.

"Wait, does he know you still like him?" SBB asked.

"No . . . ," I said slowly. "My brother said he did break up with his most recent girlfriend, but I kind of have this feeling that he might like somebody else . . ."

"Oh, like who? We are going to make you look so extra super gorgeous tonight, he won't have any choice but to fall at your feet. 'Kay?" SBB gave me her most radiant smile. "And whoever this mystery chick is, she's not going to stand a chance, right?"

I nodded happily, and then SBB finished up with mascara and lipstick. For a final touch, she put a wig on me that exactly matched hers. When I looked in the mirror I almost cried, until SBB warned me not to, because of the mascara. The butterflies were all set free in my belly. I was so glamorous, I didn't even recognize myself.

## philippa just can't muster any party

On Friday afternoon, Philippa had nothing better to do than sit with her parents during their afternoon cocktail hour. She couldn't hang out with her last best buddies, Sonya and Mickey, because Mickey hated her, and she couldn't hang out with her lesbian friends, because she was afraid they would laugh at her and tell her she wasn't a real lesbian. And she couldn't go to this party at this club that her old friend Liesel was promoting, because who knew who she might run into there.

Instead, she sat looking out the windows and listening to her father say things like, "Is this Macallan? This is damn fine scotch."

He was reading what he insisted on calling the afternoon paper, which was actually just the morning paper read in the afternoon, and her mother was updating her Rolodex. Philippa thought she might die. Luckily, ever since she had broken up with Mickey, her parents had let her drink with them, so she was sipping from a glass of her mother's favorite Pouilly Fuisse. Of course, they didn't yet know that she was a lesbian.

"Phil, you're awfully quiet today," her mother said. She didn't look up from the business card she was gluing into place.

"Yeah, I don't know, maybe I'm hungry," Philippa said without thinking. She took a fistful of hair, which she had tried halfheartedly to put in a ponytail. It had ended up sort of low and toward the side of her head, eighties style, and she now realized that her hair was also really dry looking. "Maybe I should switch shampoos," she added.

"What?" her mother said.

"You're sounding odd, Phil-bear," her dad said, peeking over his paper.

"Huh?" Philippa said.

She was wondering how she could possibly stand her parents for the next hour, much less the next year or so before she went away to college, when there was a rapping on the window frame. "Excuse me," Mickey said, and then climbed through the window. In the old days, Mickey was always doing reckless things to get in the Fradys' place, and it made her all giddy to see him doing it now.

"Mickey!" Philippa gasped. He was wearing an old cable-knit sweater with the arms cut off, with pin-striped pants and those stupid white clogs, and he was smiling.

"Hello, Fradys," Mickey said.

"Mickey," Philippa's dad said, "what are you doing here? And I want you to know that if you hurt my trellises, I'm sending your father a bill."

"Whatever," Mickey said. "I'm just here to say, first of all, Phil: You've really made me feel a lot of things lately. And some of them were not things that I wanted to feel."

"I'm sorry," she said in a small voice.

"What are you talking about, Mickey?" Philippa's mom said.

"Do your parents know that you're here?" Mr. Frady added. His favorite way of complicating the Mickey-Philippa relationship was to get the Pardos involved. That was usually when things got really psycho.

"Sir," Mickey said, "if you'll just bear with me. Phil, the thing is, there's a party tonight. And all my friends are going. And I want to go, too, but it just wouldn't be a party for me if you weren't there."

"But what about Sonya?" Philippa asked.

"Who's Sonya?" Philippa's dad asked.

"Dad, shut up!"

"I really liked Sonya," Mickey said, giving Philippa's dad a big fake smile. "That's why this is so complicated. But if I had a chance to get back with you, then there was really nothing else I could do. I had to break up with her."

"You broke up with her?" Philippa gasped.

"Yeah, I had to. I mean, plus the shit she said to you last night was totally wack."

Philippa ran up to Mickey and threw her arms around him and covered his neck with kisses. "It *was* really mean," she said eventually. Philippa shot her parents an apologetic look, and then looked into Mickey's eyes. "So, after everything, you still want to be with me?"

"Philippa, no matter how many mistakes I make, we're always just still so right for each other. And besides, it was about time you were the one making the mistake." Mickey squeezed her and lifted her up and put her back down. "I guess it boils down to the fact that I love you whether you're a lesbian or not."

Philippa's heart had a quick spasm, and she looked at her parents in time to see her mother spit white wine all over her Rolodex and her father bunch his newspaper up.

"Mickey," her mother said, "I think I misheard you. Did you say . . . *lesbian*?"

Philippa turned her expression of frozen, bug-eyed terror on Mickey. *They didn't know*, she mouthed. Philippa couldn't help but feel that her life as she had known it up till now was over. Her parents were not going to take this whole lesbian thing well.

"Oh, shit," Mickey said.

"I'll be home by midnight!" Philippa yelled. Then

she allowed herself to be pulled by Mickey down the stairs. They went hustling down, two steps at a time, and when they hit the pavement they looked up and saw the Fradys leaning out their second-story window with looks of utter incomprehension.

Mickey looked up at them, and yelled, "See ya, suckers!" Then he turned to Philippa, and said, "That was way more awesome then riding a Vespa across the Brooklyn Bridge."

"I know," Philippa said.

"Anyway, they'll get over it. They always do."

"I hope so . . . ," Philippa said. She closed her eyes and pulled even closer to Mickey.

Mickey hailed a passing cab and pushed Philippa inside. "Hit it," he told the guy, and then they peeled off. Mickey put his fists in the air, and let out a loud "Whooo-hooooo!" Then he turned a big grin on Philippa and said, "Sister, it is officially party time."

## tonight's the night, for deluded girls on the lam

"Oh, there you are!"

The giggling voices that had been ricocheting down the stairs finally appeared on the front steps. Liv looked up and saw Flan and SBB. They looked like twins, except that Flan wasn't quite as miniature, and her dress was big and gold, whereas SBB's was short and black. But they both were wearing black wigs of bob length, and they both had the artfully done faces of movie stars.

Liv smiled at them. "There *you* are!" she replied, trying to mask her irritation. She herself was wearing a strapless white eyelet dress that she had bought at Barneys that day. It had cost two thousand dollars, but it had reminded her of the dress that Liesel Reid had worn to her sweet sixteen party and was thus obviously the winner, so she had charged it to her mom's credit card and worn it out of the store.

She had superstitiously wanted Patch to be the first one to see her in the dress, but now that was ruined.

"You look amazing!" she said, stretching her big mouth into what she hoped was something like a genuine smile.

"What have you been doing out here?" Flan asked.

"Waiting for Pa— Um, never mind."

Flan stared blankly back at her. "Oh, okay," she said.

"Liv, you look really nice," SBB said. "Almost as nice as Flan. Almost, but not quite." Then she pinched Flan for emphasis.

"Um, thanks, I guess," Liv said, standing up awkwardly on her Miu Miu mules. They stood there, in the leafy evening, and smiled at one another until the car drove up.

"Hello, beauties," said the man in the black Lincoln. "Which one of you is Flannery Flood?"

Flan stepped forward and waved shyly. "That's me," she said.

"Well, hello, gorgeous," he said, reaching to the seat next to him and then extending a bouquet of mums in her direction. He smiled, and she caught a mouthful of gold teeth. "These are from DeeDee Rakoff. She's sorry she won't get to meet you tonight, but she says she's sure she'll get to meet you soon."

"These are gorgeous!" Flan said excitedly.

"Ladies, get in. The party awaits," the driver said, and then Flan and SBB piled into the car. Liv took one look back and wondered where Patch was. She imagined him in some bathroom somewhere, getting ready to go. He was probably being very serious, putting on a casual, summer-weight suit that was white (to match hers!) and brushing his sandy hair behind his ears in a belated attempt to look cleaned up. Of course, silly Patch, he wouldn't know that he looked even cuter that way—a little bit scruffy, a little bit the gentleman. Like Brad, when he belonged to Gwyneth. Maybe she would tell him later, when they were alone and . . .

"Liv, what are you daydreaming about?" SBB called from the car, and so Liv had no choice but to get in and travel to the party with a bunch of girls.

Candy was on one of those wide cobblestone streets on the far West Side that looked like it had been as empty as a movie set until the party showed up. In this case, the party meant a long line of would-be revelers who were still in high school, and a gaggle of camera people taking pictures of the red carpet. There was a twenty-foot wall, and the sounds of blaring speakers and screaming girls rising above it.

"Oh my God, look at all those people!" Flan said. She brushed the strands of fake black hair away from her face and gazed out of the car window. "Can you believe it?"

"What a great sweet sixteen, right?" SBB said.

"Where is your brother, anyway?" Liv demanded. Both of the black-wigged girls turned to stare at Liv, who felt compelled to say, "He's your brother, he should be here!"

"Come on," SBB said. She jumped out of the car and strode to the photographers. "Ladies and gentlemen!" she called. "The lady you've all been waiting for! The sweet sixteen-year-old herself! Flannery Flood!"

Flan jumped out of the car and walked up to the cameras. She went slowly at first, but the roar from the crowd and egging from the cameramen to work it and own it galvanized her, and soon enough she was turning and vamping for the guys.

"I can't believe it," Liv said. She almost felt a twinge of jealousy for all the attention her old friend was getting, but she knew that, in the grand scheme of things, tonight was really her night—her and Patch's night—so she didn't worry.

She had been talking to herself, but apparently, since she was still sitting in the car, the driver thought she was talking to him, because he said, "Eh, I seen it all before."

"Really?" Liv said, noticing the guy again. "You must have been to a lot of parties."

"Not a lot of parties. I been to a lot of press cluster-fucks. Or driven up to them, I guess." He paused meditatively. "Excuse my French."

"That's okay," Liv said. "So, do they always look like these look?"

"Yeah, because DeeDee pays the photographers to

show up and act like that. Makes it feel like a big event. Half of them probably don't even have film in their cameras."

"Really?" Liv said. "Well, thanks for telling me that." She leaned over the divide and kissed him on the cheek. "Have a good night, okay?"

Pumped with confidence, Liv strode past the cameras, and along with SBB and Flan, she went through the gilded gates and into Candy, which was not so much a club as a gigantic courtyard paved with pink stones and filled with trees that had been stripped of their leaves and decorated with candy-themed decorations. There were gigantic Skittles and jelly beans dangling from the branches, catching the candy-colored searchlights and glittering.

Inside the walls, they were playing Beyoncé and everyone was dancing and screaming. When Flan walked in, a woman with a clipboard yelled, "It's Flan!" and a cheer ran through the crowd. Or at least, the crowd of ten or so people in T-shirts that said DDR immediately surrounding them.

Flan looked flushed and excited, and she reached for Liv's hand and squeezed it. "Can you believe this?" she whispered.

"No, it's amazing," Liv whispered back. The air was thick and humid, and everyone inside the walls of Candy appeared to have a fine sheen of sweat on them.

In between the candy-decorated trees, there were topiaries decorated with little Christmas lights, so everything felt very packed and bright. They were the same topiaries that they had seen at Liesel's party last weekend, but whatever, they still looked cool.

"I can't believe this is how I get to celebrate my sweet sixteen," Flan whispered.

"Isn't this special?" SBB said. She was still standing on Flan's other side.

"Yeah," Flan said. "One question, though. Where do we go now?"

"I can answer that," the woman with the clipboard said. She was wearing Sevens and had a curtain of very straight dark hair, and she looked like she hadn't been without a cup of coffee in hand since six o'clock in the morning. "I'm Deb, from DeeDee, by the way. What you should do is go sort of toward the bar for maximum attention, and make sure you look like you're having fun. The bartender will give you your first round of sparkling apple juice on the house."

"Oh, okay," Flan said, looking mildly frightened by this news.

"And Flan?" Deb added. "The dress looks great, just don't spill anything on it, because we have to send it back to Marc's people tomorrow. Got it?"

Flan nodded, and then SBB dragged her forward into the crowd and toward the bar. "Ignore her," Liv heard SBB saying. "You'll have as much sparkling apple juice as you want."

Just then, Liv spotted Patch's friend Jonathan. He was wearing a white blazer and a black T-shirt over some stylish jeans, and he was surveying the crowd. His eyes fell on Flan for a minute, and then he looked a little confused, and his eyes kept on roving. When he saw Liv, he smiled and waved.

Liv tried to think quickly. It was possible that Jonathan knew where Patch was, but it was equally possible that he would just distract her and want to talk about Flan or, worst case scenario, he would know about that whole David slippage, and would somehow bring that up. So Liv decided that the best way to avoid that kind of negative contact was to bring maximum attention to herself. She shimmied to the center of the dance floor, where the most eyes and the most lights were on her, and started grinding with the first guy she saw.

When she looked up, she saw the slender face and wisps of dirty-blond hair that had decorated Flan's wall. Leland something or other. "Well, *awwwright*," he said, after he'd looked Liv up and down. Liv smiled right back. Because it wouldn't hurt anybody to send a subtle little signal that this was her big night, too, right? And that she was the most glamorous eighth grader on the block.

## liesel questions her fate

"Well, don't you look lovely?"

Liesel looked behind her in the mirror, and saw her mother standing in the doorway. "Thanks, Mom," Liesel said, and ran her fingers through her hair. She was wearing a little black dress with a deep V-neck that showed off the flat, pale middle of her chest.

"Are you going to see that Wildenburger boy?"

"Well, tonight's the Candy party and he's my date. So, yes, I guess I am."

"I just think that's fabulous, darling," her mother said. She moved her hand from her hip to her ear, which rattled all the gold bracelets on her wrist. The noise wasn't really that loud, but Liesel found it deeply irritating because everything her mother did lately was deeply irritating.

"Mom, I'm going to be late . . . ," Liesel said, turning to look at her mother in her all-white pant-suited glory.

"Yes, dear, you get ready. But don't forget to tell

Arno to tell his mother that they're invited for family dinner, and that my assistant will be calling with potential dates." Her mother smiled, sending ripples of elegant smile lines along her cheeks. "Ciao, darling."

Liesel had been working her butt off promoting the Candy party, and she wanted to have fun tonight, but she was still furious with Arno for messing up his big chance at fixing his image. She didn't want to hang out with him tonight, or ever again, really, much less with his whole stupid family. She thought about how little she wanted to see him all the way to the West Side. Her car pulled up in front of the Wildenburgers' Chelsea loft building, and she examined her nails until Arno had gotten in the car and given her the requisite kiss on the cheek.

"You look nice," he said.

She narrowed her eyes at him and made a guttural little noise of disapproval. "You look like one of those, what do you call them? Singer-songwriters," she said.

Arno looked down at his corduroy blazer and stretched-out-at-the-neck army green T-shirt. "I don't get it," he said.

"I mean I got you that whole Rogan outfit. You couldn't even try that for one night?" she said, and looked away. Then they both stared out the window until they got to the club.

"Oh shit," Arno said. "The media."

"What's your problem with the media?" Liesel said. She opened her compact and checked her face.

"Oh, you know, that whole Hottest Private-School Boy thing." Arno sniffed disgustedly. "The press just wasn't that nice to me is all."

"Yes, Awno," Liesel snapped, "I do know. I remember. In fact, I was trying to *fix* your whole problem with the media so you wouldn't have to go around like a wounded little puppy all the time, but *nooooo*, you couldn't handle somebody doing something nice for you. Some people just can't handle the riches fate has handed them, can they?"

"Whoa, whoa," Arno said, putting his hands up defensively. "Chill, lady. All I'm saying is what's going on out there is shallow, and I'm not just riffing, I'm saying that I have personal experience with this shit that goes so deep, maybe you can't understand it."

"Fine, Awno, whatever. For tonight, I will pretend like you didn't totally just embarrass me by not showing up at the Bowery and partying with rock stars. But this is work for me, okay? This is professional. So if you could keep your soul-searching, poetry-loving mumbo jumbo to yourself for just a little bit, I'd appreciate it. Got that?"

"Fine, whatever," Arno huffed.

Then he got out of the car, walked around it, and

opened her door. He took Liesel's hand, and together they stepped into the crowd like the super hot scions-of-art-money couple they were.

"Liesel! Liesel!" one reporter yelled. "You've been building buzz for Candy for DeeDee. Do you think it's a success?"

"You're here, aren't you?" Liesel said as she breezed by.

"Arno, does this mean you're staging a post-HPSB comeback?" another reporter yelled. Arno held up his hand to shield himself from the unpleasant questions.

"I can't believe you even had to ask," Liesel yelled. It was weird how second nature this was for her, making Arno look good. "He's so *obviously* hot again."

Arno put his arm around her and smiled rakishly at the crowd. "Whatever Liesel says must be true, right?" Arno called out good-naturedly. Then he buried his nose in her hair. For a brief moment, Liesel was reminded of the Arno she used to know—the gorgeous publicity hound Arno. Of course, that made his whole quest for depth thing that much more painful. The photographers, and the crowd pushing up behind them, let out a big "Awwwww!" They loved it, of course.

"Time for us to enjoy the party!" Liesel called. She put her arm around Arno and gave him a tug. Someone out in the crowd yelled, "Arno and Liesel, you look like you were born for each other!" And then they were swept through a wall of large men wearing all black and speaking into mouthpieces.

Liesel shook Arno off of her. "That was unpleasant," she said, pushing her hair around her shoulders.

"Tell me about it," he said.

"I mean, pretending that I even like you anymore is painful," she said.

The courtyard that was Candy was full of movement. They were playing some ridiculously catchy song that Liesel couldn't quite place—the Black Eyed Peas, maybe?—and that had gotten the crowd going. Deb, one of DeeDee's five assistants, appeared and gave Liesel a robotically quick kiss on each cheek. "Party's going fine, Liesel, good job," she said.

"Thanks," Liesel said. "Looks like all that work paid off."

"Yeah, anyway, can you pay attention to that Flan chick? I'm afraid that dress you got her is going to get messed up. And the last thing you want to do is piss off Marc's people."

"Sure, catch you later." Liesel gave her a big fake smile and turned back to Arno.

"That was real deep, hon," he said sarcastically.

"Shut up," Liesel said, dragging him toward the bar. "I need a drink, then I'll deal with you."

"Drink?" Arno said. "I could use one, too."

Liesel pushed people aside as she approached the bar, which had been specially built inside a gigantic strawberry ice cream cone. Once she'd stepped under the ice cream cone roof, she was hit by a nasty case of memory. All the bottles of energy drinks and special waters were lit up by little lights, and the bartender had a ring of candy necklaces around her neck. Liesel could smell Arno right behind her.

"What's the matter?" he said.

"This is a bar," she said slowly, "that has a policy against stiff drinks."

"What?" Arno said. "I mean, what kind of a club is this?"

Liesel crossed her arms and laughed bitterly. "This is going to be a long night," she said.

**everything is back where it's supposed to be.**
                              **for mickey, anyway.**

"Arrgh!" Mickey shouted. The music was so loud that only Philippa could hear him.

"What's the matter!" she yelled.

"This song! Every time I hear this song it gets stuck in my head for like a week!"

"Where are your friends?" Philippa yelled. She knew that Mickey was allergic to the Black Eyed Peas, and she didn't want to have this conversation with him again.

"I don't know, but they must be hiding," Mickey shouted back. "Otherwise you would be able to see them against all the pastel."

It was very pastel out there. All the people in Candyland looked really healthy and happy and like they had just washed their faces, which was weird for a nightclub. Girls on roller skates were going around with trays full of some sort of beverage.

"Oooohhh . . . hold it, hold it," Mickey said. He nodded to himself, getting into the rhythm, and then he grabbed one of the roller girls by her apron strings.

"Hey, watch it!" she yelled. She turned to Mickey with all her teeth showing, but when she saw who it was, she softened. "Mickey Pardo, long time no see."

"Hey Ula," he said, kissing her on the cheek. "What happened to your gig at Bungalow?"

Philippa stepped up and held Mickey's hand, just so that everybody was clear.

"Oh, they fired me for dancing on the bar," she said disgustedly. "And they call that a club. Now I'm in this place, what a joke! Anyway, here, enjoy." She handed two of the tall glasses from her tray to Mickey and Philippa. They were filled with a lemon-colored liquid and mint sprigs. "I'm surprised to see you here, actually," she said. "Toodles," she called as she skated away.

"That was weird," Philippa said.

"Yeah, anyway," Mickey said. He took a long pull of his beverage. "Hey, this is lemonade!"

"I guess this isn't your lucky day." Philippa giggled. "Except, you know, getting me back. Come on, let's find your friends."

They kept walking through the crowd, but they had gotten to the center where the dance floor was, and the people were so packed and enthusiastic in that area that it was hard to move.

183

"Can you believe how much these people love this stupid song?" Mickey asked.

"Holy shit," Philippa said. She had Mickey by the arm to steady her, but she still couldn't believe what she was seeing. "Look! It's Leland Brinker. I saw him at the Bitter End once, but now he's all famous."

"You still go in for that kind of cowboy junk? Even though you're a lesbian?" They both giggled, and then Mickey said, "Wait a sec, you mean that guy who's dancing with Liv?"

"Who's Liv?" Philippa wrinkled her nose.

"You know, we met her last Saturday at that party in Central Park. She's friends with Patch's little sister, she's hot . . . I mean, you're a lesbian! I'd think you would notice these things!"

"Enough with the lesbian jokes."

"Okay."

"Anyway, whoever that is, she's practically humping Leland Brinker . . . ," Philippa said. When she turned, she saw that Mickey had been distracted by his old friend Patch. They were giving each other high-fives.

"Hey, Philippa," Patch said in that totally unsurprised way of his. He was wearing a worn blue T-shirt that said ALOHA on it and brought out his eyes, and jeans that were ripped at the knee. "It's nice to have you back."

"Thanks, Patch," Philippa said.

"Aw, damn," Patch said. Philippa looked at Patch, and for the first time in all the time she'd known him, he looked kind of uncomfortable. "It's Liv," he said. "That girl is psycho. Listen, I'm going to have to bail here, but I just got a call from the guys saying they're at one of the picnic tables in the back . . ."

*"Paaaatttcchhhh!!!"* The girl who had just been dancing with Leland Brinker came bounding across several low-lying couches. She was wearing a white strapless dress that looked somehow too delicate on her, like it might be torn apart by her animal energy. She nearly knocked Patch over with the force of her hug. Then she saw Mickey and Philippa and she moved to control herself. "Hi," she said to them.

"Hi," they said back.

"Patch," Liv said in a voice that was trying to be a whisper but wasn't making it, "do they know yet?"

"Know what?" Patch said, inching away from her. "What are you talking about?"

"Understood," she said, smiling up at him like he was an underwear model on a Times Square billboard. "By the way, that thing back there with the songwriter? I was just trying to make you jealous." Then she dashed back onto the dance floor, where a cheer of "Go, Liv! Go, Liv! Go, Liv!" went up.

"Yeah, she's a wack job," Mickey said.

"You don't even know the half of it."

"Can we go see our guys now?" Mickey asked.

The three of them pushed through to the other side of the dance floor. There were a few powder blue picnic tables clearly visible, but they were all filled with people they didn't know. Finally they got to the end of the row, and saw that there was one shrouded in candy trees. They walked under the Skittles-laden branches, and that was when they saw their friends. Jonathan looked slick and carefully dressed as usual, and David was wearing a navy hoodie and jeans, and his big frame was hunched over the table. He looked like an aggressively average dude.

"Hey, Jonathan," Patch said, extending a hand to his friend. "Have you seen Flan?"

"No, man, Liesel must be hiding her in a closet for later or something. I saw her friend Liv, though, she's out there, so Flan must be somewhere."

"What's goin' on," Mickey said, reaching out a hand for Jonathan and David to slap.

"Well, David's freaking out about—guess what—girls, which is why we're hiding back here. So that's good. Oh! And this club is actually *for* people our age, so they don't serve alcohol here. Which is not nearly so bad as the suffocating cuteness of everything. Hi, Philippa, it's nice to see you," Jonathan said.

Philippa smiled. She really liked Jonathan, but sometimes he could be weirdly sarcastic about his friends' problems, which he was also obsessed with. Plus, she thought Candy was sort of adorable, and his criticizing it irritated her. "Hi, Jonathan. Hi, David," she said. "What's the matter? I thought you broke up with Amanda like a million years ago."

"Amanda?" David said. "Amanda was simple compared with this."

"You say that now . . . ," Mickey said.

"Would you all sit down?" Jonathan asked. "You're making me nervous." They all sat down. "Anyway, our David here is all in a tizzy because a starlet's in love with him and wants him to fly to Gdańsk and be in a movie with her. But he thinks that might be too *glamorous* or some ridiculous shit. He's also having a crisis of conscience because he kissed Flan's friend Liv the other night, and he thinks he might have a crush on her, too, but for some reason she's one fourteen-year-old who is impossible to get on the phone." Jonathan gave a final roll of his eyes. "That's why we can't leave this table," he concluded. "We might run into either of these girls, and we don't know what to say to either of them. I mean, David, not we. David doesn't know what to say to them."

"David," Patch said, "I don't give out a lot of advice, so you should listen when I do. That girl Liv isn't right in the head. Stay away, okay?"

"Oh," David said. He looked sort of stunned by

this advice, but like he had been touched by Patch's whole zen calm thing. "That's good. But I still kissed her. What if SBB finds out?"

"David," Philippa said, "as the only girl present, I feel I should take this opportunity to give you your get-out-of-jail-free card. It's okay. You don't have to tell, just this once. It can just be our secret. You all right with that, big guy?"

"Really?" David mumbled. "Thanks, Philippa. But the thing is, I don't know if I even want to be with SBB. I mean, maybe that lifestyle isn't for me. Not to mention, she's living in my parents' house again, which is still just as creepy and incestuous as last time, if not more so."

"And, I mean this whole thing about her being 'undercover,'" Jonathan said, with a shake of his head. "That's not real normal. Not only did she insist on wearing this wig that makes her look like Milla Jovovich in *Zoolander,* she has a Mini-Me sidekick who is dressed just like her. I saw them from behind, and it was so bizarre I just had to get out of there without saying hi to her."

"Really?" David looked like he was going to cry.

"To figure this one out, I think we all need a drink," Jonathan said. "Now, if only we could get a drink around here . . ."

"Drinks!" A tiny girl in a little black tunic thing and

a black bobbed wig careened around the corner. She grabbed hold of the table and came to a halt. It was SBB, who Philippa barely recognized from the old days when they were friends. "Do you know where we can get some? I've been looking for a drink *everywhere*." She smiled, and Philippa suddenly recognized Sara-Beth Benny under the wig. "I mean, I've been looking for you, too," she said. "David, where have you been?"

"Nowhere," David croaked.

"Well, that's just crackers. *Nowhere?*" she smiled at the table, like they were all her fans, and then she stage-whispered, "I hope you haven't been drinking too much, because we have to get on a plane tomorrow night . . . to get to the *film set* . . . in *Gdańsk*."

Philippa noticed Jonathan cringe at her emphasis. "Oh!" SBB said when she saw her. "Philippa Frady! I've been trying to run into you forever, it feels like!"

They kissed hello on both cheeks. "It's good to see you," Philippa said.

"You too," SBB said. "Anyway, forget the drinks. Don't you guys know what time it is?" There was a tableful of silence. SBB did a little twirl. "You fools!" she said gaily. "It's time to light the candles on Flan's birthday cake!"

## i'm all alone in the crowd

I have always tried not to be one of those sad sacks who spend their whole birthday feeling sorry for themselves, but it was pretty hard not to feel a little bit—okay, a *lot*—of self-pity on my fourteenth, also known as my "sweet sixteen."

I had somehow been stranded by myself at the bar, and was surrounded by strangers who appeared to be having a great time. They were squealing and dancing and generally enjoying good, clean fun under an open sky on a hot summer night and they all had faces that I recognized, either because they were high school kids who my brother knew and who had always seemed larger than life to me, or they were actual celebrities, people who Liesel had called in for the big event. And here I was, just standing still, too shy to talk to any of them. Leland Brinker was out there, dancing like a big freak, and it was starting to look pretty silly that I had ever been deciding between Leland and Jonathan in my head. Apparently all of my worst fears had turned out to be true: Jonathan was so into Liv that I had become invisible to him, and Leland, well, Leland was pretty much out of my league.

Which probably should have been obvious to me from the beginning. The me who thought she could be a big party girl seemed very, very far away at the moment, and also kind of insane.

Nobody out there knew me. I was just another girl in a gold dress, huddled by the bar and well into her fourth glass of sparkling apple juice.

I mean, why did I want to bring all this attention to myself and have a big party in the first place? It seemed ridiculously obvious to me now that I was not and never would be a party girl, whatever that means, anyway.

For the moment, though, I was just glad that Deb the PR lady had forgotten about me. Ever since she'd told me to watch my dress, I'd been paranoid about spilling something on it, and by this point in the evening, I felt like the damn thing was clawing at my skin from inside the lining.

I was also starting to suspect that certain Candy-goers had smuggled in some contraband booze, because there were definitely a few partiers who were swerving and generally looking a little more wild-eyed than sparkling apple juice would usually allow.

Seeing as how low and lonely I was feeling, I guess what happened next was inevitable.

One of those booze-smuggling jerk-offs went skidding across the pink stones and straight into me. I was knocked from my perch and out into the crowd, which graciously parted so that everybody could get a look at me sprawled on the ground. It stung a little bit, when I hit those shiny pink stones, but mostly it was just the humiliation. And the stickiness. There was definitely something sticky on the ground, and I didn't want to think about what it was doing to my dress.

"I'm so sorry," the guy said.

I looked up and immediately recognized Leland Brinker. "That's okay," I said. Well, I guess I can't complain that my celebrity crush didn't give me any birthday attention anymore.

He extended his hand and pulled me up. As I got up on two feet, I saw my wig on the floor, and felt my normal old brown hair falling down around my shoulders.

"Oh, no way!" Leland said. "You're the birthday girl, huh?"

"Oh!" I said. "Yeah, I guess I am."

"Flan, right?" he said. He kissed me on the cheek. "Happy birthday, Flan. This might be a good time to tell you I'm your surprise birthday date."

"Oh, that's great," I said, blushing. Thankfully, now that I was back on my own two feet, the crowd had gone back to not paying attention to me, so I don't think anybody noticed the pink cheeks. I couldn't believe how much cuter Leland was in person. His blondish hair was all thin and angelic, and he had really piercing blue eyes, shrouded in beautiful dark lashes.

"Hey," Leland yelled in the bartender's direction. He punctuated it with a loud whistle, like the kind you would use for a puppy. That's the kind of thing that can really break a spell, but I was still pretty impressed by his prettiness at that moment in time. The bartender gave him a disgusted look. "Two more sparkling apple juices, for me and the birthday girl!" he said.

"Happy birthday, beautiful," he said, toasting me with the sparkling apple juice. This night wasn't turning out at all like I expected, but I figured, what the hell, and downed my drink. Leland did the same. "So," he said, pumping his eyebrows at me, "sweet sixteen . . . I guess that makes you sixteen today. Big milestone," he said with a shrug, a mere lift and drop of the shoulders, that he somehow managed to make lascivious and gross.

"Actually, today is my . . ." I was about to explain to him the whole situation, but then somebody hit the OFF switch on all the colored searchlights, and I saw a glowing cake coming in my direction.

"Cake?" Patch said. "I didn't know anything about a cake."

"Yeah, well, Liesel and I thought since it was her birthday and everything . . ." SBB shrugged and smiled brightly, and then she climbed over Mickey and Philippa and into David's arms. "Hi, baby," she said.

David's friends all looked away as she straddled him and gave him a few intense kisses. When she'd had enough of that, she said impatiently, "Come on, people! It's cake time."

David and his friends followed SBB to an area hidden behind planted trees, where Candy staffers were busily washing glasses and generally freaking out about the insanity out there. In the center of all this activity was an incredibly realistic-looking cake, in the shape of a miniature baby elephant.

"Oh my God," Philippa said. "That cake is crazy cool!"

"I know, right? Liesel was planning on a real elephant but then Candy called last night and said that elephants weren't allowed in the club, and since she's representing them and everything, she couldn't really bully them. So we thought of this. Usually, they only do wedding cakes, but it turns out this particular pastry chef is a fan."

"Fan of what?" Mickey said. "Clubs for underage people?"

"No," SBB said, her face falling a little bit. "A fan of my show."

"I got that," Jonathan said.

"Thank you, Jonathan," Sara-Beth said. She continued to put candles into the cake, and as she did she felt David's eyes on her. That was the kind of rapport they had. She lifted her eyes to him and winked. David, as usual, looked somewhat freaked out by the overwhelming attraction. That was when she realized that David wasn't wearing the suit that she'd bought him. It didn't matter, really. He always looked great, even in a simple hoodie and jeans. *Especially* in a hoodie and jeans.

"Hey, SBB," Patch said, "I think you've got too many candles there. Flan is only fourteen today."

Sara-Beth looked up at him and then batted the naysaying away. "I know, but it's her sweet sixteen. So I put sixteen candles on the cake."

"Don't you think that's kind of weird?" Jonathan asked.

"Oh, whatever," SBB said. "Nobody counts the candles anyway."

"Okay," Patch said. "Whatever makes Flan happy. You guys ready?"

He picked up the cake, and everybody followed him. They moved into the center of the Candy courtyard like a small army of Flan-adoration. SBB gave the DJ the signal and then he turned off the searchlights and lowered the music. The crowd parted for them, and they moved forward, first Patch and SBB, then Jonathan and David, then Philippa and Mickey. When Sara-Beth caught sight of Flan, sitting next to Leland Brinker at the bar, she started to sing. In halting voices, they filled that courtyard with a rousing version of "Happy Birthday to You."

Something had happened to Flan's wig, but she looked beautiful with her hair falling down and her gold dress slightly askew. As SBB crooned, "And many more . . ." she even thought she saw Flan's big eyes get all mysterious and wet, like she might cry.

"Don't cry," SBB said, coming right up to her with Patch and the big elephant cake. "You have to blow out your candles. And besides, your crush is right there." Flan looked at her and gave three furtive little shakes

197

of her head. "No, over there," Sara-Beth said, pointing a slender arm in Jonathan's direction. She turned to look at him, to make sure he was actually in the direction she had pointed, and she saw that he was frozen in the middle of saying something to David and that the color had gone out of his face. She looked back at Flan, and decided that she would figure out later how to tell Jonathan that Flan had a crush on him. "Well, don't just stand there! Blow the candles out."

Flan smiled weakly, leaned forward, and blew out all but one candle. As she looked at the last wayward candle, one big tear collected on the rim of her eye and then dropped.

"Hey, Flan," a female voice out in the crowd yelled. "Why are you crying? Is it because you have a secret?"

Flan jerked up, and SBB looked around trying to see where the voice had come from. "Who said that?" SBB yelled.

"What, are you trying to deny that there's something a little off about this sweet sixteen party?" the same voice yelled. There was a smattering of laughter across the crowd, and then it grew. Pretty soon it seemed like everybody was laughing. And then it got worse.

"We paid to get in here!" one of the partygoers yelled. "And we want our sweet sixteen-year-old to really be sixteen!"

A chant went through the crowd. It took SBB a

second, but then she realized that they were doing a call and response thing. "How many candles, Flan?" one person would yell, and the crowd would chant, "Fourteen, fourteen, fourteen."

"This is absurd. These people are *soooo* literal-minded," SBB said to their little group, but especially to Flan. She couldn't believe that there were this many people in the world who would be willing to pay to get into a club and cared about sweet sixteens this much. "Are you okay, hon?" she asked, and then decided that if Flan tried to talk she was just going to straight up burst into tears. "Come on," she said to Patch, who was looking pretty concerned about his little sister, "we've got to get out of this lame, kids-only party and go to a real club."

Patch looked down at the cake. "Totally, but what am I going to do with this?"

"Oh, give it to me," SBB said impatiently. She took the elephant cake in her hands, and used the whole weight of her body to throw it out into the crowd. Chocolate cake and gray frosting burst all over several of the loudest chanters, and one girl was fully knocked over. This only riled the crowd up more, though. "Come on!" Sara-Beth yelled. "Flan, I'm sorry your party got ruined like this. But all of my birthdays get ruined, so maybe it's a good thing! Anyway, I'm getting out of here. Are you coming with?"

Flan nodded, and then turned to Jonathan. "That whole thing, though, about the crush . . ."

Jonathan fished for Flan's hand and caught it. "If it turned out you were interested in getting back together, that would be like a birthday present for me," he said. "But right now, we just have to get the hell away from this place before we all catch the lame."

"Okay," Flan said.

"And by the way? You look way better without the wig," he said. "Because you look like you. And you is what I like."

Flan smiled and blushed and didn't care that she was blushing. "Thanks," she said.

"This is beautiful," SBB said, glad to see her friend back with the guy she liked. "Now, can we just go?"

"SBB, there's something I have to say," David said. He was looking at his oversized athletic shoes and shuffling a little bit.

"Yeah, well say it!" SBB shrieked. She usually felt protected by David, but she had just thrown a gigantic cake at an angry crowd of people, and she felt like the protective thing for him to do right now was to get them the hell out of there. "This isn't exactly a family therapy session here! We're surrounded by hostile birthday party guests!"

"I know, I know. It's just that when I saw you getting all excited about Flan's birthday and doing normal shit like lighting the candles on her cake, I realized that you were a real person . . ." David put his hand on his forehead. "That didn't come out right . . . but anyway, I think I might be in love with you, and, well, I guess the point is that I want to go to Gdańsk." David inhaled deeply. "With you."

"Well, of course you do," Sara-Beth said, throwing her arms around him. "And whatever you were trying to say, I'm sure it was very sweet."

"Okay," David said.

The "How many candles, Flan? Fourteen, fourteen, fourteen," chant had become deafening. It had been time to leave five minutes ago, but when they turned to leave none of them could figure out which way the gates were. And they were surrounded on all sides by angry sweet sixteen celebrants, pounding their fists into their hands.

## it's not for nothing they call liesel no-nonsense

"This sweet sixteen is a farce!" screeched a girl with very straight brown hair. She was wearing low-riders and a lavender shrug over a dark purple tank. Liesel caught a glint of braces when she looked at her. "We paid thirty dollars to get into the sweet sixteen party of a fourteen-year-old! Refund, refund!"

"Deborah," Liesel said, grabbing her DDR coworker by the access pass hanging around her neck on a plastic chain. "Who the hell is that? And who let her in?"

Deb cocked an eyebrow and looked at her clipboard. The chanting filled the room now, which was weird, because these people weren't even drunk. Maybe a whole room of people fueled by energy drinks wasn't the safest idea, either. "That would be Mona Brill, from Flan's—ahem—eighth-grade class. She was on the list *you* gave me."

"Well, what's her problem?" Liesel asked.

"I don't know, I hear fourteen-year-olds often harbor

immature resentments," Deborah said. "And by the way, Lies, this doesn't look good on the résumé."

"Oh, shut up, Deb," Liesel said. She gave a mighty push to the unfortunate girl in front of her and strode over to the DJ booth. "Mind if I use this?" she said, taking the mike that the DJ had been using to make announcements with. "Good. Listen up, everybody!" The feedback reared up through the sound system, but it was no match for Liesel's voice. "You're all being really lame, and, I'd like to add, sort of uncouth."

"Farce! Farce! Farce!" the crowd chanted up at her.

"Farce?!" Liesel hurled the word back at the crowd of self-righteous idiots. "You call this a farce! All of you loved my sweet sixteen party, remember? Remember? The Central Park Boat House, shrimp cocktail to die for? Yeah, you remember. You loooooved *that* sweet sixteen. And I turned *seven*teen four weeks ago!"

A collective gasp went up from the room and then everybody got very hush.

"You people gross me out," Liesel said. "In fact, I'm so disgusted with you that I'm quitting the public relations biz. Obviously, none of you appreciate what I do for you anyway. You don't deserve my buzz. Buh-bye a-holes!" Liesel tossed the microphone into the DJ's lap and strode down through the stunned and silent crowd. "Come on, posse," she said to the little group forming a protective wall around Flan. Then she turned toward the entrance, and the wall of people parted, making a clear path all the way out of Candy.

Once they got outside, Flan ran up to Liesel and smiled. There was sadness in her eyes, but also relief, and the beginning of happiness. She was wearing a white blazer over her gold dress. "Thank you, that was so nice of you," Flan said.

"Those people are all pathetic," Liesel said. "I would have done the same for anybody."

"Well, still. Thanks," Flan said earnestly. "And I want to be the first one to tell you that I think this Marc Jacobs dress got messed up. Before the cake disaster, I had this . . . other disaster, and I think there's something sticky on the back."

Liesel smiled. "Don't worry, dahling. Dry cleaning will probably get it out, and as far as I'm concerned, that dress belongs to you. I'm never going back to DeeDee's, so Mawc's people can cry all they want to."

Flan laughed and hugged Liesel. Then she stepped back, to be with Jonathan.

"So, where are we going?" Jonathan said.

"Let's go to Lotus," SBB said. "It's my last night in New York, before I fly to Europe, and I'd really like to break my contract in style."

"I'll go anywhere they serve alcohol," Liesel said, and then laughed heartily at her own joke. "And Lotus, as I know from personal experience, serves all kinds of alcohol." She looked down the dark street, lit up by pools of orange street-lamp light and all the taxicabs lining up to take people from Candy and then around the city to more exciting and authentic places. Out from the pack of yellow cars, she recognized her Lincoln. "There's my car," she called. "Who's coming with me?"

"I am."

Liesel looked over at the guys and saw Arno stepping out from the group. His guy friends all watched as he put his hand on her hip and guided her into the car. "Awno, I really don't think . . ."

"We'll meet you at Lotus," Arno called over his shoulder before climbing into the car. "Could you just drive around for a minute?" Arno said to the driver.

The driver turned into the street. Liesel shook back her hair, sucked in her cheeks, and said, "Awno, can't we wait till tomorrow to break up?"

Arno raised his faintly exotic eyes to her and held her gaze through the wisps of his bangs. "I don't want to break up."

"Well," she said, and exhaled definitively through her nose.

"I brought you this." Arno reached into his coat, and took out a small object wrapped in wax paper. Liesel touched it and realized it was soft. "Open it," he said.

Liesel unfolded the package and looked down on

what appeared to be a PB&J. "Ew, did you have this in your coat all night?"

"Yeah," Arno said softly. "In case you got hungry later on."

Liesel giggled despite herself. "That's pretty cute, Awno."

"Tell you the truth, the way this night was going, I didn't think I was going to get to give it to you."

"Yeah," Liesel said.

"But if you're really giving up on all that PR craziness, then I'm in," Arno said. "I want to be your boyfriend—and your fate."

"All right then," Liesel said, putting her PB&J into her Kate Spade clutch. "Now can we make out the way our old shallow selves would at this point in the evening?"

Arno smiled, slowly at first, though soon it was a wicked, teeth-bared, ready-for-anything grin. Liesel shot across the backseat and landed on his neck.

The driver drove around the block a few more times, and when he dropped them at Lotus, Arno jumped out of the backseat, held the door for Liesel, and then helped her to the curb. She did a little twirl into the night air, pulling down her skirt, and then they walked to the door like the ridiculously hot couple they were.

Which was when they met up with the bouncers, and heard two unfortunate phrases.

"Is that a hickey?" followed shortly by, "Yo, I'm going to have to see some ID."

## i'm the new me, just like the old me, but a little bit better

I stood there on the street in front of Candy feeling all ragged and pure in my ruined Marc Jacobs dress with my ex-boyfriend/best friend/ new love interest at my side. There was the faint sound of car horns from off in the distance, and there was just a hint of ocean water on the breeze. All the cabs had lined up, like we were at the front of the line at the airport or something, and they were just waiting to take us where we wanted to go. I pulled Jonathan's jacket around my shoulders and smiled up at him.

"Let's go to Lotus," he said.

"Yes, please," I said.

But you didn't think we were just going to go quietly into the night, did you?

As we turned to take our pick of cabs, an Escalade screeched up to the curb, or more like up *on* the curb. When it came to a stop, its right tires were well onto the sidewalk. A woman in a black velvet tracksuit with her blond hair up in a twist stepped down from the Escalade, and when she saw me she said, "Oh, Flan, thank God."

"Hi, Mrs. Quayle," I said.

"Where's Liv?" she said.

I tried to smile innocently, and turned back to look at the club. "I think she's . . . ," I started to say, but then I saw the Candy gates open again, and Liv came bouncing out of the club, her long, horsey legs in front of her.

"Flan!" she said. "Are you all right?" She did look genuinely concerned, although also kind of manic—maybe she'd found somebody with a secret flask, too?—and her mouth was hanging open. I jutted my head in the direction of her mother, and when she saw her she didn't, to tell you the truth, look all that surprised. "You found me," she said.

"I sure did, honey," her mother said, shaking her head. "Your father's so mad, he can't even get out of the car. You were supposed to fly to London, not New York. What in hell is wrong with you?"

"I gotta be me, Mom," Liv said.

"Oh yeah? Fine. But it's gone on long enough.

Get in the car, we're putting you on an airplane tonight. You're just going to have to say bye-bye to all your friends right now. You'll get to see them next year in school anyway, because I'm keeping you here in New York and on a tight leash for the next four years."

Liv stood there for a minute, and then she turned and dashed away from her mother. For a minute, I thought she was trying to run away for real—we all did—but then I saw that she was just beelining for my brother. Everybody else got all shocked and gaspy looking, but he just stared at her, calm and cool like usual.

"I guess it couldn't be," Liv said. She put her hand over his mouth, and continued: "No, don't speak. There's nothing to be said anyway." Then she threw her arms around his neck with such enthusiasm that it actually looked like he might get hurt, and kissed him, the way they do in the movies, with the back of her head twisting around in all kinds of animated directions.

Just when our jaws were all starting to get sore from hanging open, Mrs. Quayle stepped forward. "Liv," she said quietly but forcefully, "enough."

Liv turned around and shot her mom a pained expression. "I'm coming, Mother," she said hatefully. Then she turned back to Patch. "Just know I will always love you," she said, and then she turned and followed her mother to the car.

We all watched as the car pulled away, and then we turned and stared at Patch, to make sure he was okay. Mostly in the head.

"What the hell was that?" Mickey said finally.

"Hey, man," Patch said with a drop of the shoulders and a twinkle of a smile, "who am I to stand in the way of a girl and her dreams?"

"Amen," Jonathan said. "Now really, can we please go to Lotus?"

We crammed into two cabs, Sara-Beth and David and Jonathan and me into the first one, and Patch and Mickey and Philippa in the next. Once we were on the road and away from Candy, never to return, I turned to Jonathan and said, just to broach the topic, "That was pretty crazy, huh?"

"Yuh," he grunted in agreement.

"I mean, how could I even think that you like, liked her?" I felt Jonathan and David snap to attention and turn their eyes on me, but I just gazed out the window and waited for some answers.

"What? I never liked her," Jonathan said laughingly. "David was the one who . . ."

David elbowed Jonathan—I knew, because

Jonathan was sitting between David and me and I felt the impact. "That's insane!" David said. I realized that he was acting all huffy because SBB was in the front. Jonathan and I both looked, and we saw that she was talking to the cabdriver.

"Oh my God, you're from Gdańsk?" she was saying. "I'm about to go make a movie in Gdańsk. So what should I bring, for summer there? To wear, I mean."

"No clothes in Gdańsk," the cabdriver was saying. "No money! Nobody have clothes in my country."

"Really? They wear nothing?" SBB said. "Wow . . . that's hot." She giggled, and then continued to lob questions at him.

"I didn't like Liv," David hissed at us when he was satisfied that SBB wasn't listening to us. "I was just confused."

"Oh, come on," Jonathan said. Then he looked at me. "That was why I called you the other day asking for her, because David wanted me to."

"Okay, okay," David said. "Maybe I liked her a little bit, but mostly I was confused."

"But *you* never liked her," I said to Jonathan.

"Hell, no!" he said.

"Good," I said. Jonathan took my hand and

kissed it, and then I knew for sure that there really never had been anything between Liv and him.

Our cab got to Lotus first, and we jumped out and into a frenzy of activity. At the center of it all, I saw Liesel yelling at some big bouncer who was like three times as wide as she was.

"I just forgot it," she was saying. "Is that a crime? But I work for DeeDee Rakoff, and if you don't let me in . . ."

"Uh-oh," I heard Mickey, coming up behind us from the curb, say. "I guess they're doing that old-fashioned twenty-one-and-over-only thing again."

I felt my stomach rock, because even though none of us were over twenty-one, I was *especially* under twenty-one. "Hey guys," I said meekly, "maybe we should just—"

"No way," SBB said. She pulled off her wig and glasses and handed them to me. The Sara-Beth Benny of celebrity weeklies and TV and infamous tantrums appeared and strode up to the bouncer. She placed her hand on her hip and then cocked it.

"Excuse me," she said. "Do you know who I am?"

"Yes . . . ," he said slowly. He turned to look at one of the other giants guarding the door.

"Oh, whatever, let them in," the other guy said.

"I'm going to need my entourage," SBB said.

"Yeah, yeah," the guy said.

"And a nice, private area," she continued.

"Okay, okay," the guy said. Then he muttered something into his walkie-talkie.

"Come on, gang!" SBB called, and we all held our heads up as we walked into the crowd, which was full of people bumping and grinding and yelling along with the music. It was a scene. We were led to a private banquette, though, and once we'd all crammed in—Jonathan, David, SBB, Liesel, Arno, Mickey, Philippa, and my brother, Patch—everything seemed to settle, and I knew the fireworks were over for the night. I was with people who didn't care if I was a glamorous party girl or not—in fact, I think they might have preferred just regular old me.

"Any chance you've got a birthday cake back there?" SBB asked the waitress.

"Yeah," Liesel said, "and birthday candles? Fourteen of them."

The waitress gave us a doubtful look and said, "Well, I'll check."

Everyone looked so beautiful and sparkly

there, in the low club light, that I couldn't help but smile. The waitress returned, looking bemused, with a small chocolate cake lit up with fourteen pink birthday candles. "Apparently this just arrived, compliments of somebody named February Flood," she said as she set it down on our table.

Jonathan waved his hand to stop all that horrible singing from happening again, and then he said simply: "To Flan. Happy birthday."

"Happy birthday!" everybody chorused as I blew out the candles.

I still couldn't stop smiling. There were cool people everywhere, but I had all the people I needed right there around me.

Don't miss the next book from J. Minter, *Inside Girl*, coming soon!

From now on, it's all about Flan! Flan's starting high school at Stuyvesant, an *enormous* public school in downtown Manhattan. She's a little nervous about the big change, but it'll be worth it. She'll do anything to become more than just Patch's little sister. But convincing her new friends at school that she's worthy of their normal girl clique becomes unexpectedly hard when three unforgettable guests arrive at the Perry Street townhouse and absolutely refuse to leave.

Sara-Beth Benny is having boy troubles and housing troubles, plus she's dodging the paparazzi *and* her manager. Flan's bedroom is the perfect hideout!

Liesel's parents are in Paris and her house is being renovated. Everybody's after her to plan their parties—but all she wants is to help Flan find just the right boy.

Philippa totally hates her parents for ruining her relationship with Mickey. The only way to nurse a broken heart is in the company of friends!

But Flan's houseguests must remain secret. Can she keep these glamorous girls hidden, find the right high school boy to date (no, we don't mean Jonathan!), and get the girls at school to like her for the right reasons?

While you wait, check out the latest at www.insidersbook.com.